BARNABAS

A Historical Novel on the Life and Times of a First Century Christian.

Yann Opsitch

BARNABAS: A HISTORICAL NOVEL ON THE LIFE AND TIMES OF BARNABAS, A FIRST CENTURY CHRISTIAN.

ISBN (print paperback) 979-8-9908025-0-6

ISBN (hardback) 979-8-9908025-1-3

ISBN (ebook) 979-8-9908025-2-0

Published by Timeh Publications

Yann Opsitch Author

www.yannopsitch.com

Dedicated to my Grandchildren:

Robin and Emma

Faustine, Agnès, Marie and Constance.

Contents

JERUSALEM

Palace of Annas and Caiaphas
Herod's Palace
The Fortress Antonia
Temple
Upper City
Lower City
Pool of Siloam
Mount of Olives

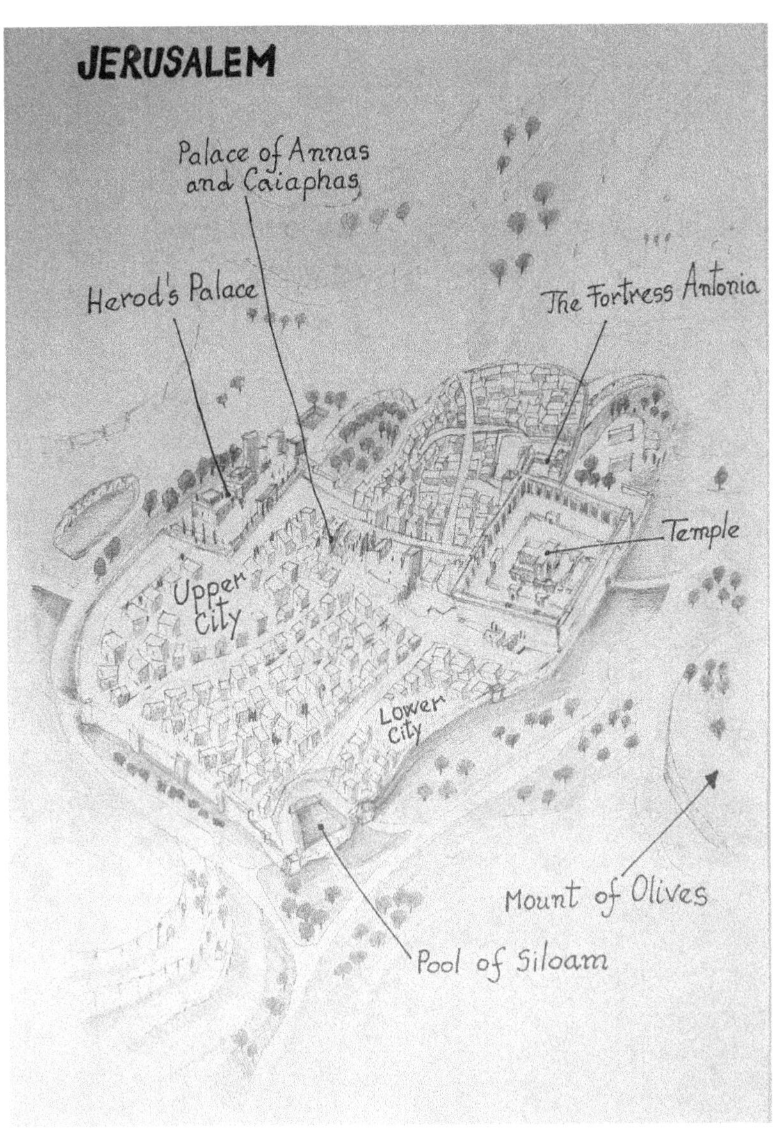

Paul's first missionary journey with Barnabas and Mark.

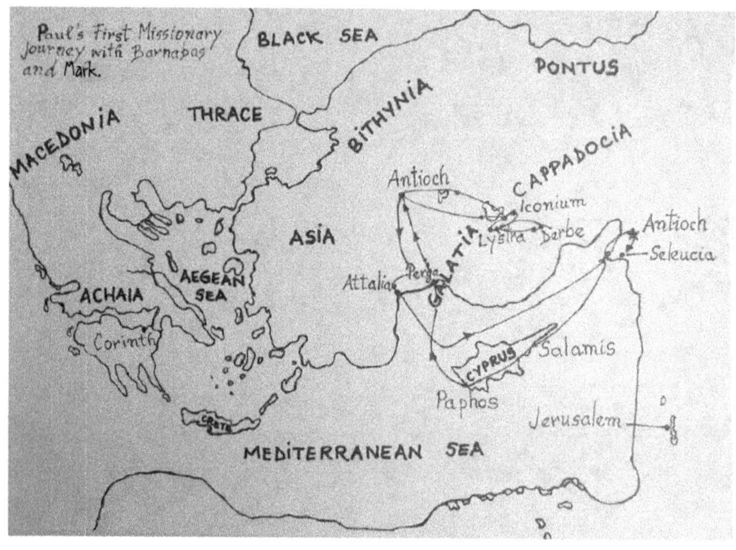

I

A LETTER FROM LYSTRA

In the Spring of 48 AD (during 8th year of the rule of Claudius) Barnabas and the apostle Paul evangelized major cities of southern Galatia. When they came to the city of Lystra, Cyrillius was the high priest of Jupiter in that city. This priest to a pagan god had a young servant by the name of Erastus. After the preachers left the city, this young man was deeply moved by the life and teachings of the new Lystra Church, and he became a Christian. He later was granted the status of a free man.

Erastus became a preacher and teacher of the Lystra congregation.

On the 2nd year of the rule of Domitian (83 AD) — thirty-five years after his conversion — Erastus of Lystra and two other younger disciples, Justus and Lucius, traveled during the month of May to Cyprus in order to meet with Barnabas and convey greetings and love from Lystra to the "Son of encouragement". They were also bringing funds for the needs of the recent converts of Salamis who had lost their livelihood when they abandoned the worship of Dionysios (Bacchus), the god of wine and winegrowers.

Three months earlier, Erastus had written the following letter to Barnabas and the Church in Salamis:

To our dear Barnabas, servant of the Lord and to our brethren in Salamis, grace and peace from I Erastus and the Church in Lystra.

Thirty-five years ago, many here in Lystra still remember your visit to our city along with the apostle Paul. At the time I was the young servant of Cyrillius, the high priest of Jupiter. After your departure the brethren in Lystra continued faithfully to teach and worship our Lord and I became a disciple of the Lord Jesus.

I am now a preacher and teacher for the congregation. We have been informed of the hardships endured by the Church in Salamis at the hands of the priests of Bacchus. We have heard that some of our brethren who have vineyards and make wine have lost everything upon orders from the governor of Cyprus who is a worshipper of Bacchus.

The brethren in Lystra as well as Iconium have gathered funds together to bring to the Salamis congregation in order to help our brothers and sisters who have lost everything because of their faith in Jesus. I will be traveling to Salamis with Lucius and Justus to bring this contribution on behalf of the brethren.

Lord willing, we plan on arriving to Salamis the early part of August of this year. It will be a great joy for us to meet with you and your wife Sarah as well as our brethren in Salamis.

May God's peace and strength be showered on your life as you serve the Lord in Cyprus and remain faithful to His calling and to the Hope of eternal life.

Erastus, evangelist to the church of our Lord in Lystra.

II

THREE ENVOYS FROM LYSTRA

Erastus, Lucius and Justus, each one loaded with a heavy bag, stood ready to leave the ship as soon as it would dock inside the recently built Roman harbor to the north Salamis.

"That was not such a bad trip" exclaimed Justus, stepping down from the ship. He was clearly relieved to have reached Cyprus since he was more prone to seasickness and had feared the over 28 hours on the Great Sea. "These days we can be grateful to God anytime we arrive at our destination" replied Erastus as he himself felt relief to be able to walk again on firm ground.

The three men were carrying a good amount of drachma and some gold hidden in two of the heavy bags they carried. They knew that thieves were constantly on the move especially around ports and ships. They had prayed fervently for weeks that nobody had any idea of the amount of drachma they were carrying as well as some gold — enough to feed several families for a couple of years!

The gates of Salamis were only a mile away. Having walked through Salamis and towards the northern side of the town, out into the country, they finally reached the humble house where Barnabas and Sarah lived and where the Christians met for worship.

The house stood on a small elevation about two miles from Salamis and a short distance from the governor's villa and the temple of Bacchus built on the same grounds. The impressive villa was not the main residence of the wealthy governor since the seat of Roman power was on the other side of Cyprus in the city of Paphos, 90 miles away.

As they were coming closer to the humble dwelling of Barnabas, and ready to knock at the door, it was still early in the morning. Barnabas had been praying and reading for the past hour. In his hands he held the most recent copy of the letter to the Ephesians written by the apostle Paul when he was emprisoned in Rome and already copied as well as circulated among the churches.

The Son of encouragement was deep in his thoughts reading the great insights of Paul's short letter to the Ephesians. He heard as in a dream the knock on the door. Sarah had been preparing breakfast and at once went to the door, opened it and with a big smile let the three very tired men come into the house.

Sarah and Barnabas had been expecting their arrival for the past couple of weeks and were overjoyed by their safe arrival.

As he entered the house, Erastus thought he would see an old man bent down by age, but Barnabas looked much younger and stronger than he expected. Barnabas whose name means "son of encouragement" was not only a pillar of the faith but was known as a very strong as well as tall man in physical stature. Erastus was overwhelmed with feelings of gratitude to be in the presence of such a servant of the Almighty and preacher of the Gospel of Jesus the Christ who had traveled with the "apostle to the Gentiles".

The three men sat at the low table in the main room that served as kitchen, dining room and fellowship hall to the local church. Having warmly greeted the three men and offered water to them, Barnabas started sharing with them the content of the letter to the Ephesians he had been reading that morning. He finished saying to his guests, "May God's grace be eternally upon you and all who love our Lord Jesus Christ."

Silence followed these words. Each one in the room was plunged into deep thoughts about the implications of what the apostle had written from Rome a few years ago and prior to his death at the hands of Nero.

Sarah rose up and brought the bread, lamb and cooked vegetables to the table. As they ate a late breakfast, the three brethren brought news to Sarah and to Barnabas from the Lystra congregation and the area churches and even from churches farther away, Colossea, Ephesus, Smyrna, Pergamum and several others.

Erastus as well as Lucius and Justus asked Barnabas if he would tell his story of how he came to the faith and what happened since. They were eager to hear the story of Barnabas, of how being a Jew and a Levite he had believed in Jesus of Nazareth as the Messiah of Israel.

Thus, they spent the entire day listening to the amazing personal testimony of the "Son of encouragement". It is this testimony we are recounting now.

III

THE STORY OF BARNABAS

1. BUSINESS IN JERUSALEM

It was not the first time for Joseph, the Levite from Cyprus, to land on the shores of Syria only a few miles away from the great city of Antioch.

Sailing for a few days on the Great Sea (The Mediterranean) from Cyprus, his homeland, to Syria was not a new experience for the 35 year old merchant of olive oil, who also happened to be a member of the Jewish priesthood. In ancient Israel the priests served in the temple and received their livelihood from the contributions stipulated by the law of Moses. But Joseph lived in exile and had inherited lands and a farm from his father close to the town of Salamis on the island of Cyprus.

As he stepped off the ship on solid ground after a rough sail of two days and one night, the young man took in a deep breath and started walking, looking forward to his third visit that year to Jerusalem. Barnabas was taller than most men and gave the impression of great physical strength; but he was the kindest of individuals, known for being a peacemaker even at a young age.

It was the beginning of Spring and Joseph would greatly enjoy the climate of the Coast of Syria as he would travel further south and into the Holy Land. The way to Jerusalem would follow the coast for a couple of days and after that would come the slow ascension into the mountains of Judea to the beautiful city of David.

Joseph reached Jerusalem Friday evening just before Saturday, the day of Jewish rest.

He stood at the door of his uncle Ben's modest but well-built home on the upper part of the city of Jerusalem. As the thick wooden door opened, he smelled the delicious meal Hannah had prepared for his arrival: a stew of cabbage and mutton meat with fine herbs.

"Joseph" exclaimed Ben stood smiling, "We are so thrilled to see you."

The next day the weather was clement as Joseph climbed up on the roof of his uncle's house to enjoy the end of the Sabbath day. As the noises of the city faded away, he was praying and meditating on some of the Psalms of the Passover feast.

As he watched the activities of the street below, Joseph noticed a group of men and women, as well as young people and even children, entering a spacious house on the opposite side of the street. There could have been almost a hundred of them. He thought to himself *maybe this is a wedding meal or a family reunion.*

Later that evening at the dinner table Joseph wanted to know the nature of the special event or the celebration, going on in the house on the other side of the street. Hesitantly at first, Ben answered the question of his nephew and said, "Last year, on the day of *Shavouot* (also called Pentecost) something unusual happened in the temple. Hundreds, even thousands of our Jewish brethren, mostly from the diaspora, were immersed into the waters of the pools of Siloam. They did this after a man called Peter spoke in the temple about Jesus of Nazareth who had taught many but had been crucified."

Why would our own brethren go through this act of purification? This is the strangest thing I have ever heard coming from our Jewish brethren, thought Joseph. "What can you tell me about this man Peter and this other teacher, Jesus of Nazareth?" asked Joseph.

Ben mentioned some other events that had happened during the past four years, including some of the rebellions against the Romans led by those called "zealots" crushed at the time by the governor Pilate. There was also this man John who preached and also immersed followers in the Jordan. Many in Israel saw him as a prophet of God. This John had been captured by the soldiers of Herod Antipas and imprisoned because he had condemned the king's unlawful marriage to his brother's wife Herodias. This preacher John was eventually beheaded.

Having said these words, Ben seemed suddenly reluctant to continue this narrative and started inquiring about his nephew's business and how things were going on in Cyprus. Barnabas understood that he did not wish to pursue this conversation.

Two days later Barnabas returned to Cyprus but this time his thoughts were full of the events of the past few days and the discussions with his uncle Ben about what had happened in Jerusalem over the recent years.

Watching from the deck of the boat, he enjoyed the smell and sounds of the sea which was exceptionally calm. According to his uncle Ben one of his cousins, whose name was Mark, had in fact, become a follower of this man Jesus who had died on a Roman cross.

Barnabas knew Mark very well and had often stayed in his home while visiting Jerusalem. *Why would Mark be following a dead teacher? Especially one who had died the death of a criminal and had been rejected by the highest religious authorities in Israel?*

As he traveled back home, Barnabas already knew he would need to return to Jerusalem to spend some time with Mark and ask the many questions raised by his uncle's account about John the baptizer and Jesus of Nazareth.

2. MARK

As soon as he reached Cyprus, Barnabas wrote a letter to his cousin Mark. Barnabas concluded his letter by asking Mark if they could meet early in the fall when he would travel back to Jerusalem for business.

John Mark, as he was known, had been a disciple of Jesus almost from the start of Jesus' ministry. He had met the apostles and knew Peter and John well. At the time Mark was beginning to write what later would be called a "Gospel", an account of what Jesus had done and taught. Three other such accounts or Gospels would be written by Matthew and John, two of Jesus' apostles and Luke the doctor who also wrote the Acts of the Apostles and traveled with the apostle Paul.

Mark was not married. He and his mother Mary lived on the west side of the city, close to the Temple grounds. The house was larger than most other homes in that part of the city of David. The upper room where the family would gather could easily hold fifty people. Barnabas returned to Jerusalem the early part of the fall. This time he was the guest of Mark and his mother.

One evening after dinner and the usual sharing of family news, Barnabas wanted to ask Mark his first questions. The early fall was cool and still warm enough for them to sit on the flat roof top of the house. "Mark" said Barnabas with eagerness in his voice, "as I wrote to you last Spring, something happened at the house of my uncle Ben which has troubled me ever since. As I was resting and praying on the rooftop of the house towards the end of the Sabbath day and the start of the first day of the week, I saw a group of men and women with some children all coming together and meeting in the house I could see on the other side of the street. Why would our brethren gather on the evening of the Sabbath?"

Barnabas continued, saying: "Last Spring uncle Ben mentioned to me how at *Shavouot,* a little over a year ago, many of our brethren were immersed into the pools connected to the temple. I did not understand what this could mean. My uncle himself had no answers to give to me except he talked about this man named Peter who preached on Pentecost and also the teacher he followed whose name was Jesus of Nazareth."

"My uncle also mentioned another man whose name was John and who preached several years ago. He was called the Baptizer. He immersed those from Israel who came to him and who confessed their sinful ways, turning to God with humility and seeking his forgiveness."

Barnabas finished with these words, "I do not understand the meaning of these events. Uncle Ben mentioned that you consider both this John and Jesus as having been sent by God with a message for our people."

Mark had listened intently to his cousin's questions and remarks. It took him some time to gather his thoughts. With great calm, mixed with rejoicing that his cousin was willing to talk about all of this, Mark spoke to Barnabas and replied saying, "In the past few years great things have happened here in Jerusalem and for our people. These events have changed my life, the life of my mother, as well as many of my friends from Jerusalem and even from Judea and Galilee.

"The events concerning Jesus of Nazareth lasted over a period of three years, starting with John who immersed in the Jordan those who came to him with repentance towards God. This John preached saying, 'Someone is coming soon who is greater than I am—so much greater that I'm not even worthy to stoop down like a slave and untie the straps of his sandals. I baptize you with water, but he will baptize you with the Holy Spirit!'"

"Mark" said Barnabas, interrupting his cousin, "Was John doing like so many others have done in recent past and promising the appearing of the Messiah, the savior and ruler of Israel and even of the nations? If the Messiah has come, why are we still in bondage to Rome and nothing seems to have changed even here in the city of David? If the fire of God's judgment has come on His enemies as preached by John the Baptist, and the Messiah has brought the fire of God's judgment on our enemies, why are the Roman conquerors, their idolatry and pagan ways still covering our land?"

As he looked at the rooftops of the city and could distinguish the high walls of the temple not far away, knowing that even the Roman governor was ruling right next door with an iron hand, Barnabas said to himself with sadness; *How could Mark seem to be so full of certainty, even joy? How could he believe the promises of God had come to pass and think that freedom and peace can now be fully enjoyed? Nothing seems to have changed for Israel.*

At that point Barnabas remembered to ask Mark about the gathering of Israelites on the day following the Sabbath. What was the meaning of this gathering on such a day? What did these Jewish brothers and sisters commemorate on such a day?

"Joseph", said Mark smiling, "You are welcome to join Mary and I tomorrow at sunset and see and hear for yourself. Maybe what you will hear and see will help you understand what has happened and why we believe the Messiah has come to save us."

3. THE BREAKING OF BREAD

Mark, his mother and Barnabas got ready to attend the Synagogue close by and a short distance from the temple. The word "synagogue" comes from the Greek language and means "gathering" or place of worship.

At the time of Barnabas' visit with Mark, a lot of the Jewish life close to the temple grounds centered around this synagogue. The building was not very large and could contain at the most about a hundred and twenty participants. Benches were lined up against the walls facing a podium from where the elders and heads of the Synagogue would speak or read. Neighbors and their families met at the Synagogue for communal meals, for school and also to collect and distribute any needed help.

At that time in Jerusalem there were 394 synagogues. During the three great festivals of Passover, *Shavuot* and *Sukkot,* everyone would try and go up to the temple from far-away lands. Many of the Jews offered their sacrifices regularly at the temple but also attended the local synagogues for prayer, Scripture reading and teaching. At that time the Temple worship was controlled by the powerful and wealthy Sadducees who did not believe in the resurrection or even angels.

Sabbath was always a great opportunity for the Jewish community to have meals together, to talk and be instructed either at home or at the local synagogue. This would be a unique Sabbath for Barnabas since he had been invited to attend in the evening the local church. Several of the men and women, young and old, and even children who followed the teachings of Jesus of

Nazareth were to meet in a house located in the lower part of Jerusalem, over two miles from the Temple grounds.

It was almost getting dark outside when about thirty guests arrived for the meeting and packed the small house. Mark had explained to "the son of encouragement" how Jesus of Nazareth before his crucifixion had instructed his disciples to break bread as a sign of covenant with God, "²² As they were eating, Jesus took some bread and blessed it. Then he broke it in pieces and gave it to the disciples, saying, "Take it, for this is my body." ²³ And he took a cup of wine and gave thanks to God for it. He gave it to them, and they all drank from it. ²⁴ And he said to them, "This is my blood, which confirms the covenant between God and his people. It is poured out as a sacrifice for many. ²⁵ I tell you the truth, I will not drink wine again until the day I drink it new in the Kingdom of God." (Mark 14.22-25)

Barnabas was struck by these words quoted at that meeting. *How could a human sacrifice fit into any covenant with God? How could the blood of a human being give access to the blessings of the Kingdom of God or his forgiveness? In this case, what would happen to the priesthood if animal sacrifices would be of limited value?* Moreover, the circumstances and means of Jesus' death through the cross were most shocking for any Jew or even Gentile. Everyone knew that the Romans crucified only men of the most violent behavior; either thieves or murderers who had tried to raise up a sedition against Rome.

As Barnabas listened to the reading of the Scriptures and songs and as he witnessed the sharing of the bread and of the cup, he wondered how any Jew could think that the Messiah, the glorious king and descendant of David, could be put to death like a criminal or a thief; he even wondered: *Is this was a different way of celebrating Passover?* However, this could not be the case since it was not the period of the Passover feast.

Mark sat facing the assembly and beside him were three other men who appeared to be about in their mid-thirties. Barnabas was surprised to find such young men in charge of this assembly, barely the age of being young rabbis. How could they be recognized as credible teachers? What was so unique about them?

Before the start of the celebration, Mark had presented them to his cousin as Peter, James and John. He had briefly explained that Jesus had chosen them to be with him and had called them "apostles".

Peter stood up first and said, "Jesus was arrested, beaten and condemned to the cross under the rule of Pilate. His death on the cross was not the result of a human decision or simply the rejection of his teachings, but the very means by which God had from all eternity chosen to reconcile us to himself. Jesus of Nazareth was publicly endorsed by God by doing powerful miracles, wonders, and signs through him. God knew what would happen, and his prearranged plan was carried out when Jesus was betrayed. With the help of lawless Gentiles, he was nailed to a cross and died. But God released him from the horrors of death and raised him back to life, for death could not keep him in its grip." (Acts 2.25-28).

Peter ended his speech and sat down. This was followed by a moment of silence.

Peter had also quoted Psalm 16 and Barnabas knew the text. He had often wondered how David could speak of himself as having conquered death even though his tomb was right there in Jerusalem and the resurrection had not happened.

Peter the apostle had pronounced words that truly shook Barnabas to the core when he said, pointing to James and John, "God raised Jesus from the dead, and we are witnesses of this." He realized for the first time that this faith in Jesus of Nazareth, risen from the dead, was not simply a belief founded on some biblical texts or tradition, but a belief founded on witnesses to events that had happened not long ago.

After John and James had also spoken, songs were sung, and the assembly shared in the bread that was broken for all and the cups of wine that were passed around. Prayers were made. Those gathered together greeted each other with a holy kiss and departed.

As the meeting drew its end, Barnabas had so many questions he could not wait to ask his cousin and his mother.

The worship he had just witnessed centered around the person of Jesus of Nazareth with readings from our Scriptures and songs and with the sharing of the unleavened bread and the fruit of the vine.

How could this be? How was this in keeping with the Torah and all the instructions about the priesthood and sacrifices, about the entire meaning of the Scriptures? How could this be what God's people had been waiting for in the person of the Messiah, the anointed one, the King of Israel?

It was already late that evening when they reached Mark's home and entered the house. Barnabas did not wait to speak up. Addressing his cousin, he said nervously, "I am so concerned about all of this. And why the sharing of unleavened bread and the fruit of the vine when it is not even Passover? How is this not contrary to the stipulations of our Torah and our holy feasts?"

"My dear Joseph," responded Mark "We can answer all these questions, but it would be important for you to also speak with the apostles you met briefly. A lot of this is not only about the Torah or the writings of our Prophets or our Psalms, but about events witnessed by these three men and many others. I encourage you to meet with two or three of these disciples of Jesus since the law teaches us about the importance of two or three witnesses to establish a fact."

Then and there Barnabas decided that he would need to speak personally with these apostles.

4. APOSTLES OF JESUS

Barnabas needed to return to Cyprus to solve some issues having to do with his farm and business. A private meeting with several of Jesus' apostles occurred two months later.

This meeting happened during the feast of Tabernacles or Tents (also called *Sukkot*, the last week of September.

Barnabas was a little over thirty years old at that time, the age Jesus received baptism from John the Baptizer and started his ministry.

Sukkot is the seventh and last feast the Lord God taught his people Israel to observe on the 15th day of Tishri. It is one of the three feasts when Israelites who are eager to "appear before the Lord" in the place he had chosen (Deuteronomy 16.16). The feast is mentioned throughout the Tanakh and many important events took place at *Sukkot*, like the dedication of Solomon's temple (1 Kings 8.2). In the book of Ezra, it was during Sukkot that those who returned from exile gathered to rebuild the temple under Joshua and Zerubbabel (Ezra 3). Nehemiah records that the Torah was read by Ezra (Nehemiah 8). Those who had gathered confessed their sins and repented of their sins.

Sukkot began five days after the Day of Atonement when the fall harvest had just been completed. One could feel the joy of those in Jerusalem and those coming from far away as they celebrated God's provision through the forty years in the wilderness after the exodus from captivity, remembering also to be thankful for the present harvest they enjoyed.

Before leading Barnabas to his meeting with the apostles, Mark spent some time recounting important aspects of the preaching of Jesus and what happened from the time of Jesus' baptism by John the Baptist up to his death on the cross.

Barnabas would learn later from Jesus' disciples that it was during *Sukkot* that the Lord had said these famous words in the Temple, "If anyone thirsts, let him come to me and drink. He who believes in Me, as the Scripture has said, out of his heart will flow rivers of living water". We learned from John that these words had to do with the great gift of the Holy Spirit the Messiah would pour on God's people, "Now this he said about the Spirit, whom those who believed in him were to receive, for as yet the Spirit had not been given, because Jesus was not yet glorified." (John 7.37-39).

Mark told his cousin that Jesus had chosen twelve of his disciples to be his apostles and witnesses to Israel and the nations. One of them, Judas, had betrayed Jesus on the night of his arrest in the garden of Gethsemane and had been replaced by one named Matthias who had accompanied Jesus since the baptism of John until his ascension and was numbered among the apostles. (Acts 1.15-26).

Mark explained to his cousin that these twelve apostles witnessed Jesus' three years of teaching, and his many miracles.

Early in the morning, after almost a one hour walk from Mark's home, Barnabas and his cousin reached the humble house on the south of the city of David where the meeting had been planned.

Barnabas had already briefly met Peter, James and John. This time James was with his brother John and Peter with his brother Andrew. Matthew also was present.

After a coded knock on the door of the house, Mark and his cousin entered the small room that served both as kitchen and main dining and living area.

"Greetings my dear Mark," exclaimed Andrew as he opened the door to the two guests, "Seven of us apostles are here to meet with you and your cousin Barnabas, and we welcome both of you into the home of our brother Samuel."

As he said those words, Mark and Barnabas walked towards the low table in the middle of the room and sat with the seven men, including Samuel their host. After offering some wine to the two visitors, Samuel informed Barnabas that he had been among the seventy sent out several times by the Master to preach to Israel.

As he looked around, Barnabas felt uneasy. He was comforted by the presence of Mark. A multitude of questions had flooded his mind for several months, to the point that he was at loss to know where to begin the conversation.

It was Peter who spoke first and mentioned the fact that John and his brother James as well as himself and his brother Andrew had been at the Jordan river when John the Baptizer preached and where crowds came to listen to him and receive a baptism of repentance for the remission of their sins" (Mark 1.4). Matthew, a tax gatherer, had been called later by Jesus to be an apostle.

As he listened to Peter, Barnabas thought *Peter and these other men looked at this John as a prophet sent by God.* Barnabas thought deeply about the implications of this belief that John was a prophet. *Had not all of God's prophets spoken and had not the Scriptures been completed hundreds of years before the preaching of this John?*

As if knowing the thoughts of Barnabas, the apostle James spoke up and reminded Barnabas of the words of Malachi and Isaiah who had prophesied about the "messenger" who would prepare the way for the coming of the Messiah. This messenger was John the Baptist who quoted the prophets as he preached to Israel, including the political and religious leaders :

> "Look, I am sending my messenger ahead of you,
>   and he will prepare your way.
> ³ He is a voice shouting in the wilderness,
> 'Prepare the way for the LORD's coming!
>   Clear the road for him!'"
> (Malachi 3.1; Isaiah 40.3).

Continuing to speak, James told everyone present how Jesus of Nazareth had come to be baptized by John. But John did not want to immerse Jesus in his baptism of repentance and even said to him, """I am the one who needs to be baptized by you," he said, "so why are you coming to me?" But Jesus said, 'It should be done, for we must carry out all that God requires. 'So, John agreed to baptize him." (Matthew 3.14,15)

This part of the account was astounding for Barnabas. *This Jesus of Nazareth had no sins to repent of?*

James went deeply into the Scriptures and reminded everyone that the Messiah would be called "holy" and would come as a pure lamb to offer his life for the people and even for all peoples of the earth. The Messiah prophesied about in the Hebrew Scriptures would be perfectly sinless and would offer his life for the forgiveness of sinners. He was described by Isaiah as one who would bear the sins of many and make intercession for transgressors. (Isaiah 53.7, 12).

In these conversations with five of Jesus' apostles, Barnabas started seeing how in the Scriptures the Messiah would suffer for the sins of the people, would be put to death but would also overcome death. These were important truths from God which matched so perfectly the testimony of these apostles of Jesus.

The great obstacle to faith for Barnabas had to do with the crucifixion of Jesus and why the Romans would put to death a man who was neither a thief, a murderer or one who had raised up a sedition against the Roman authorities?

John spoke up and described everything in detail from the garden of Gethsemane to Jesus' death on the cross of which he was personally a witness. The Roman procurator Pilate did not want to crucify Jesus knowing full well that there was no legal reason to have him crucified. That is when Pilate gave the authority to the high priests to have Jesus crucified and "took water and washed his hands in front of the crowd. "I am innocent of this man's blood," he said. "It is your responsibility!"

Four hours had already passed since they had begun talking.

It was time for the men to have lunch, which had been prepared by Samuel's wife and his older daughter. While eating, the apostles inquired about Barnabas and his family. The Levite explained the history of his father and ancestors who after the captivity had been able to move from Babylon to Cyprus, closer to the Holy Land. They had not come from captivity utterly destitute and had been able to buy land and plant a good number of olive trees in several of the fields as well as vines in another. Joseph had been blessed by God and the hard labor of his ancestors with wealth and a beautiful family.

During the meal Barnabas was still thinking about John the Baptist and his death at the hands of king Herod as well as the death of Jesus at the hands of the Pilate and the High Priest. He remembered that prior to Herod the Great, the high priesthood had been hereditary, but with Herod the appointments had become terminable and no longer confined to one family. The authority to appoint high priests lay then at first with Herod and after that with Archelaus whose kingdom included Judaea and Jerusalem. Sometimes the governor or procurator would appoint the high priest. Thus, Caiphas was appointed high priest by governor Valerius Gratus and his successor Pontius Pilatus retained Caiphas in this position and it was under Caiphas that Jesus was condemned to death and crucified. After the appointment of Annas by Herod, the High Priests would often place their sons or relatives in key positions in the Temple hierarchy such as Temple treasurer and Temple supervisor or captain. It was a known fact that the relatives of the High Priest received a handsome salary and were decked in fine linen and expensive jewelry. Widows in these high priestly families received generous pensions straight out of the Temple treasury.

These were the thoughts of Barnabas while they shared a delicious meal and also discussed family and business issues.

Barnabas also wanted to know how Jesus taught and what he taught. He was young even to be called Rabbi. He was not numbered among the older men of Israel during his ministry or famous as the well-known Rabbis such as Gamaliel. He did not have the reputation of Hillel or Shammai who preceded him as teachers in Israel.

As the conversation continued, Peter mentioned that not too long ago the Sadducees were angered at the preaching of the resurrection of Jesus in the temple. As the rulers and elders inquired about their preaching, Peter had spoken these words and even quoted the prophet Isaiah, "Rulers and elders of our people, [9] are we being questioned today because we've done a good deed for a crippled man? Do you want to know how he was healed? [10] Let me clearly state to all of you and to all the people of Israel that he was healed by the powerful name of Jesus Christ the Nazarene, the man you crucified but whom God raised from the dead. [11] For Jesus is the one referred to in our Psalms, where it says,

> 'The stone that you builders rejected
> has now become the cornerstone.'

[12] There is salvation in no one else! God has given no other name under heaven by which we must be saved." (Acts 4.8-12)

As he listened to Peter, Barnabas thought: *the Sadducees do not believe in the resurrection of the dead while the Pharisees do believe in it.*

James spoke up and recounted how these leaders of Israel only a few months ago were surprised by the boldness of Peter and John who were common and uneducated in the rabbinical teachings of the elders and Scribes. They then "recognized that they had been with Jesus" (Acts 4.13). On this occasion these leaders warned Peter and John "to speak no more to anyone in the name of Jesus". (Acts 4.17,18).

Barnabas was surprised to hear how both Peter and John replied with great boldness to this warning and said to these leaders, "Do you think God wants us to obey you rather than him? [20] We cannot stop talking about everything we have seen and heard." (Acts 4.19,20).

After a period of silence, Barnabas looked at the men around the table and shared his concern over the keeping of the Torah, the law of Moses: "Brethren, ever since I have learned about these events, first through my cousin Mark and now through your personal witness, I have wanted to ask the question of what Jesus taught concerning the law and concerning Moses. We know what happens when our people abandon the commandments and start living like their pagan neighbors. The history of our people is a witness to the danger of living as Gentiles without the law, of becoming lawless."

After another moment of silence Matthew simply spoke the words of the sermon Jesus preached on the mount at the beginning of his ministry. As he listened to Matthew, Barnabas was touched at how much that sermon seemed to call everyone to a great degree of consecration to God, even beyond those who serve God day and night in the temple or others who give themselves to the study and teaching of the Law.

Matthew reminded the group of men of Jesus' words, [17] "Don't misunderstand why I have come. I did not come to abolish the law of Moses or the writings of the prophets. No, I came to accomplish their purpose. [18] I tell you the truth, until heaven and earth disappear, not even the smallest detail of God's law will disappear until its purpose is achieved. [19] So if you ignore the least commandment and teach others to do the same, you will be called the least in the Kingdom of Heaven. But anyone who obeys God's laws and teaches them will be called great in the Kingdom of Heaven.[20] "But I warn you—unless your righteousness is better than the righteousness of the teachers of religious law and the Pharisees, you will never enter the Kingdom of Heaven!" (Matthew 5.17-20).

Barnabas thought, *What Matthew is saying about Jesus' teachings reminds me of Rabbi Hillel, who had been a teacher of Israel not long ago.*

There was much debating among the Rabbis as to the importance of Hillel as compared to Shammai. It was in fact believed by some of some of the well-known teachers that the teachings of the house of Shammai, very strict and unbending and thus especially intended for the era of the Messiah, while the teachings of the House of Hillel, full of compassion and care were needed for an imperfect world full of sin and deceit. The Pharisees also had many rules and traditions which come from this very strict interpretation of the Torah and considered necessary in order for God's people to avoid the ways of the pagans.

Barnabas listened intently to Matthew, and it seemed that Jesus' teachings were not an encouragement to neglect the requirements of the law but a better and fuller way to fulfill the law. While Moses had taught the ten commandments "Do not commit adultery", Jesus went beyond this and taught about the necessity of purifying one's heart, [27] "You have heard the commandment that says, 'You must not commit adultery.' [28] But I say, anyone who even looks at a woman with lust has already committed adultery with her in his heart. [29] So if your eye—even your good eye—causes you to lust, gouge it out and throw it away. It is better for you to lose one part of your body than for your whole body to be thrown into hell. [30] And if your hand—even your stronger hand—causes you to sin, cut it off and throw it away. It is better for you to lose one part of your body than for your whole body to be thrown into hell." (Matthew 5.27-30)

The law condemned murder, but Jesus' teachings would lead to a fuller realization of what this commandment required by dealing with the deep-rooted sin of anger and added these words, 23 "So if you are presenting a sacrifice at the altar in the Temple and you suddenly remember that someone has something against you, 24 leave your sacrifice there at the altar. Go and be reconciled to that person. Then come and offer your sacrifice to God." (Matthew 5.21-25).

Barnabas understood the central place of the commandment found in Leviticus, "Love you neighbor as yourself" which was often understood to be a Jewish neighbor and especially the one going to court with another. But Jesus even applied this to "enemies", 43 "You have heard the law that says, 'Love your neighbor and hate your enemy. 44 But I say, love your enemies! Pray for those who persecute you! 45 In that way, you will be acting as true children of your Father in heaven. For he gives his sunlight to both the evil and the good, and he sends rain on the just and the unjust alike. 46 If you love only those who love you, what reward is there for that? Even corrupt tax collectors do that much. 47 If you are kind only to your friends, how are you different from anyone else? Even pagans do that. 48 But you are to be perfect, even as your Father in heaven is perfect." (Matthew 5. 43-48)

The discussion continued all afternoon until the setting of the sun.

When Barnabas and Mark walked out of Samuel's house and towards the higher sector of Jerusalem the night had fallen.

Multitude of stars could be seen flickering and twinkling in the sky. As this sight, he remembered the words of the Psalm:

> [1] Praise the LORD!
> Praise the LORD from the heavens!
>   Praise him from the skies!
> [2] Praise him, all his angels!
>   Praise him, all the armies of heaven!
> [3] Praise him, sun and moon!
>   Praise him, all you twinkling stars!
> (Psalm 148.1-3)

5. MARK'S GOSPEL

The peaceful feeling brought about by the night had calmed his heart. Waking up in the morning, however, Barnabas immediately felt the burden on his heart concerning what he had heard from his cousin and these other disciples of Jesus of Nazareth.

Well awake after only a few minutes of this new day, Barnabas remembered that his visit to Jerusalem would last two more days and started breathing more deeply, somewhat relieved by the prospect of more time to be able to continue the conversation about these amazing events.

As he sat that morning at the table with Mark and his mother, Barnabas was comforted by the familiar surroundings of the house. Both his cousin and his mother seemed always so joyful and at peace. *How could that be? What did he not understand or simply not know that brought about this joy in their lives?*

"Mark" said Barnabas taking a piece of flat bread, "You mentioned to me that you felt compelled to write an account of all these events about Jesus from the time of John the baptizer to his crucifixion and even the amazing accounts I have been hearing from you and your friends about this man coming back alive from the dead. Please tell me more about these events."

"Barnabas, about six months prior to Jesus' baptism, John came baptizing in the inhabited areas of the land, preaching a baptism of repentance for the forgiveness of sins. John also preached and proclaimed to the people that they were witnessing the fulfillment of the words of Isaiah as well as Malachi. The later prophet had said: "Look! I am sending my messenger, and he will prepare the way before me. Then the Lord you are seeking will suddenly come to his Temple. The messenger of the covenant, whom you look for so eagerly, is surely coming," says the Lord of Heaven's Armies." (Malachi 3.1). The former had also prophesied of God sending one to prepare the way for the coming of the Lord. (Isaiah 57.14)."

"And what happened once Jesus was baptized by John?"

Mark took some time to collect his thoughts and responded. "During the first months of his ministry Jesus preached throughout all of Galilee in all the synagogues, casting out demons. (Mark 1.35-39)."

"What was the message Jesus of Nazareth preached in the Synagogues? What Scriptures did he refer to in his teachings?"

"When Jesus preached in the synagogue of Galilee, he quoted from the prophet Isaiah:

> The Spirit of the Sovereign Lord is upon me,
>   for the Lord has anointed me
>   to bring good news to the poor.
> He has sent me to comfort the brokenhearted
>   and to proclaim that captives will be released
>   and prisoners will be freed.
> (Isaiah 61.1,2; Luke 4.18,19)

Barnabas had heard these Scriptures read in the Synagogue at Sabbath during certain periods of the weekly liturgy. After Mark had spoken the Levite wondered, *If this Jesus of Nazareth was the Messiah, this means he was the King of Israel promised in the Scriptures such as in the second of our Psalms. In what way did the teachings and work of Jesus show us the glorious king of Israel described for example in this Psalm or so many other prophecies about our Messiah?*

As he was thinking about all of this, Barnabas continued with his breakfast. After a cup of goat milk, the Levite looked again towards Mark and his mother and asked them about this question of the kingship of the Messiah, the descendant of David promised in the prophets.

Mark answered and explained to his cousin how Jesus preached throughout Galilee and proclaimed the Good News of the rule of the Messiah saying, "[15] "The time promised by God has come at last!" he announced. "The Kingdom of God is near! Repent of your sins and believe the Good News!" (Mark 1.15).

Barnabas understood that this description of Jesus' teachings corresponded to the expectations of Israel as far as the Kingdom of the Messiah. The significance of Galilee was never at the center of our religious and national lives of the people. He did remember that the prophet Isaiah prophesied of the light that would shine in the land of Galilee at the coming of the Messiah: "Nevertheless, that time of darkness and despair will not go on forever. The land of Zebulun and Naphtali will be humbled, but there will be a time in the future when Galilee of the Gentiles, which lies along the road that runs between the Jordan and the sea, will be filled with glory."

As if knowing the thoughts of his cousin, Mark quoted from the prophet Isaiah, saying :

> "²The people who walk in darkness
>   will see a great light.
> For those who live in a land of deep darkness,
>   a light will shine."
> (Isaiah 9.1,2).

Although Barnabas had heard these Scriptures all of his life since childhood, he had not thought much about the fact that in the great prophecies of Isaiah, the nations, the Gentiles were of great concern to God and his work of salvation. This would happen when the Messiah would appear, the one on whom "the Spirit of the Lord" would come, the "anointed one" of the great God of Israel. (Isaiah 61.1).

Indeed, Mark was right: according to the text of the prophecies of Isaiah, the Messiah would preach to Israel and bring good news to the poor; he would bind up the brokenhearted and proclaim freedom to the captives. He would proclaim the year of God's favor and comfort those who mourn. (Isaiah 61.1,2).

For some reason Barnabas wanted to immediately talk about the topic of the resurrection of Jesus. It was as if there was something about this aspect of Jesus' work that would bring a better understanding to these ancient prophecies.

Mark answered Barnabas by explaining that the apostles chosen by Jesus testified not only that he rose from the dead after three days in the tomb of Joseph of Arimathea, but also that they met with the resurrected Jesus for forty days after his resurrection. During those forty days, Jesus taught them more about the Kingdom of God and the salvation of Israel and the nations. He ordered them to preach the Good News and to be his witnesses beginning in Jerusalem, to all of Judea, Samaria and to the ends of the earth. (Luke 24. 44-49; Acts 1.8).

Mark and Barnabas discussed basically all day long and well into the night,

Some of the burden Barnabas had felt in his heart seemed to become lighter as the day went by and the discussion continued. What was first a burden for the Levite was little by little replaced with a greater sense of curiosity and interest concerning all these events.

Barnabas pondered the fact that the House (teachings) of Rabbi Hillel and (teachings) of the House of Shammai disagreed on many things but agreed concerning the glory to be brought to Israel through the work of the son of David, the Messiah. According to Shammai, it was only when Messiah would come that the descendants of Israel would be able to conform their lives to all the requirements of the Torah.

So much of what Barnabas and his cousin talked about that day was about a Messiah rejected and despised, even crucified like a criminal. The Son of encouragement was greatly troubled by this. It seemed that the Messiah would not be despised and dishonored this way.

As the night fell on Jerusalem Barnabas still had many questions about the Scriptures and God's people.

He was faced with a great paradox: this man Jesus who was crucified like a criminal had clearly called his people and all men to a holy life and to living out the two great commandments found in our in the books of Deuteronomy and Leviticus: "Listen, O Israel! The LORD is our God, the LORD alone. [5] And you must love the LORD your God with all your heart, all your soul, and all your strength." (Deuteronomy 6.4,5)

Even more surprising, *according to Mark and the apostles, Jesus who had gone through death on a Roman cross had come back to life three days later.*

This apparent victory over death, witnessed by so many, was for the Levite the most striking part of the testimony of these men from Galilee. This resurrection from his cruel death could not be explained away. No human being could survive the cross and even the beatings and floggings he had endured.

Barnabas still had a lot of questions and wanted to better understand all these events. Without his resurrection, Jesus would just be one more individual among thousands, whose life was ended by the cruel cross of the Romans. Especially, he wanted to talk with John who was the only one at the cross with the mother of Jesus and other women. And he also wanted to talk with Peter who had been with Jesus as an apostle from the time of the Baptist and had been called by the Lord to be a "fisher of men".

According to Mark, there were now thousands in Jerusalem who had come to faith in Jesus of Nazareth and had been immersed in his name. Mark also mentioned to me that just recently Peter and John had been thrown in prison by the magistrates and the Sadducees who teach that there is no resurrection of the dead. The Levite believed in the resurrection of the dead as also did the Pharisees. He could not understand why the leaders of the temple would throw men in jail for merely teaching what had been taught for several generations by the Pharisees such as Rabbi Gamaliel.

He needed to talk to John who had just been freed from prison. According to Mark, the great Council with Annas and

Caiphas, as well as John and Alexander of the high-priestly family, had just ordered the two apostles "to speak no more or teach in the name of Jesus." (Acts 4.13-22).

6. PETER AND JOHN

That evening Barnabas met Peter and John in the lower part of the city at the home of one of Jesus' disciples whose name would not be known by the high priest's family and the leaders of the temple.

Their host and his family were among those who had no influence, power or official title. They had come to faith a few weeks after the Pentecost when three thousand had heard the preaching of Peter and had been immersed in the name of Jesus.

It was a small house — a house like so many others in the city of David made of mud bricks and with a rough stone foundation. The humble dwelling had two rooms, a front room with an awning and a private room behind it. There was also a small storage room for food at the back, especially jars of oil and olives. There was very little wood as part of the construction since only the wealthy could afford wood. There were two windows in the main front room; they were high and close to the ceiling. The weather was warm, and the windows were covered with a lattice.

The three men could have met in the small courtyard but for safety the men chose to remain inside the main room for their discussion. Peter and John spoke with a strong Galilean accent quite distinct from the Judean dialect spoken in Jerusalem that Barnabas was used to.

Barnabas had continued to think about what he had heard from these two apostles of Jesus and others and even from his cousin Mark concerning the raising back to life of Jesus after his crucifixion.

Jesus, who seemingly had displayed so much power in so many ways, had let himself be mocked and struck, spat upon by Roman soldiers, Gentiles. Barnabas had not ceased to meditate on the words of his cousin: "[16] The soldiers took Jesus into the courtyard of the governor's headquarters (called the Praetorium) and called out the entire regiment. [17] They dressed him in a purple robe, and they wove thorn branches into a crown and put it on his head. [18] Then they saluted him and taunted, "Hail! King of the Jews!" [19] And they struck him on the head with a reed stick, spit on him, and dropped to their knees in mock worship. [20] When they were finally tired of mocking him, they took off the purple robe and put his own clothes on him again. Then they led him away to be crucified." (Mark 15.16-20).

Mark had also mentioned that John was the only apostle of Jesus present at the crucifixion.

After the usual greetings by their host and his wife, the three men sat down to eat a light evening meal. Barnabas was surprised how Peter looked so young. The fisherman greeted the Levite warmly recalling their former encounter when they had broken bread together and drank of the cup.

While the three men ate, Peter and John talked about Jesus and the events that happened since his resurrection and ascension. Peter explained how on the day of Pentecost in the temple court he had preached the Gospel of Christ for the first time. He mentioned the healing of the man who had been lame since birth. Peter testified about Jesus and salvation, reminding those who were listening of Moses' promise, recorded in the book of Deuteronomy, "[22] Moses said, 'The LORD your God will raise up for you a Prophet like me from among your own people. Listen carefully to everything he tells you.'[23] Then Moses said, 'Anyone who will not listen to that Prophet will be completely cut off from God's people.' (Acts 3.22,23; Deuteronomy 18.18,19).

Barnabas spoke up and asked Peter, "Do you mean that when Moses prophesied about God "raising up" a prophet, this was already about the resurrection of Jesus?"

"Yes" answered Peter, "The Scriptures prophecy clearly about a suffering Messiah but also about a victorious Messiah over his enemies and over death."

Barnabas asked Peter and John if Jesus himself had said anything concerning his resurrection prior to his death.

"I am so glad you asked this question, Joseph" replied Peter. "In fact, the Master spoke about his death and resurrection a number of times during our travels and in his teachings."

"I remember an important statement by the Master" added John.

John continued to speak and said, "At the very beginning of his ministry after his baptism and the first Passover of his ministry, Jesus went into the temple and rebuked all the money makers and merchants. He 'made a whip from some ropes and chased them all out of the Temple. He drove out the sheep and cattle, scattered the money changers' coins over the floor, and turned over their tables. Then, going over to the people who sold doves, he told them, "Get these things out of here. Stop turning my Father's house into a marketplace!"

"Having done this the leaders and teachers asked him, 'What are you doing? If God gave you authority to do this, show us a miraculous sign to prove it.' And the Master responded to this request of a miraculous sign saying, 'Destroy this temple, and in three days I will raise it up.'" Outraged, these leaders replied to him, "It has taken forty-six years to build this Temple, and you can rebuild it in three days?"

"But, continued John, when Jesus said 'this temple' he meant his own body. After he was raised from the dead, we remembered he had said this, and we believed both the Scriptures and what Jesus had said." (John 2.15-18).

When John mentioned the Scriptures, Barnabas thought to himself, *unlike the Sadducees, my own father and all our family believe in the resurrection of the dead.*

During this long conversation, John also mentioned how Jesus had talked about his coming death as the good shepherd struck and killed who gives his own life for his sheep, adding these words from the Master, [17] "The Father loves me because I sacrifice my life so I may take it back again. [18] No one can take my life from me. I sacrifice it voluntarily. For I have the authority to lay it down when I want to, and also to take it up again. For this is what my Father has commanded." (John 10.17,18).

After the long explanation given by the apostle John, Barnabas addressed Peter wanting to know if Jesus had at other times mentioned his coming death and his resurrection.

"Yes" replied Peter, "this was something the Master talked about a number of times." He continued, explaining how the Pharisees asked the Master to perform miraculous signs, but he told them they would only be given the "sign of Jonah".

Jonah had been sent by God to preach repentance to the city of Nineveh, thrown into the sea but swallowed by a great fish and found alive.

At these words of Peter, the Levite remembered the words of the prophet Jonah as he was in the belly of the great fish "For You cast me into the deep, into the heart of the seas, and the floods surrounded me; all Your billows and Your waves passed over me… The waters surrounded me, even to my soul; the deep closed around me; weeds were wrapped around my head. I went down to the moorings of the mountains; the earth with its bars closed behind me forever; yet You have brought up my life from the pit, O Lord, my God" (Jonah 2.3-6).

Barnabas knew that Jonah went to Nineveh and the city repented of its sins. The inhabitants had heard the preaching of Jonah but had also heard about the miraculous sign of this prophet of Israel being delivered from certain death through God's intervention after being thrown into the sea.

Peter also mentioned Jesus' teachings which occurred at Caesarea Philippi. This Gentile city was also called *Paneas* because the god Pan was worshipped there – a city built by Philip the Tetrarch at the sources of the Jordan near the foot of Mount Hermon.

According to Peter, it was at Caesarea Philippi that Jesus asked his disciples, "Who do men say that the Son of Man is?" The disciples responded that it was believed Jesus was Elijah, or John the Baptist, even Jeremiah or some other prophet.

But continued Peter the Master then asked the question, ""But who do you say I am?"

Who really was Jesus? was the question Barnabas had asked himself every day for the past few months. *Was he an evil man or a false prophet as he had heard some complain about him?* But, thought Barnabas, *how could this be if the people saw him as Elijah, Jeremiah or one of the prophets* — and in this way being considered in Israel among the greatest heroes of God's people?"

Peter continued to speak, saying: "When the Master asked: And who do you say that I am?" I responded: 'You are the Messiah, the Son of the living God.'" (Matthew 16.16).

Peter added these words, "It was then that Jesus taught us that my answer was not a human idea or opinion but the very revelation of God. He said to me, 'You are blessed, Simon son of John, because my Father in heaven has revealed this to you. You did not learn this from any human being.'"

This discussion about the identity of Jesus as the Messiah troubled the Levite greatly while at the same time produced in his heart a greater sense of curiosity concerning Jesus of Nazareth and his claims.

As Barnabas was thinking about this, Peter continued the conversation with the surprising words the Lord told him, "You are Peter and upon this rock I will build my church, and all the gates of Hades will not prevail against it".

The Levite knew that "hades" or the "gates of hades" had to do with death itself. The words of Jesus meant that the church Jesus talked about would be a building of the Lord and would not be threatened by any foe, even death itself. It would in fact be founded on rock. His thoughts went quickly to Scriptures which described the Messiah as the rock of Israel, the foundation upon which the faithful could build their lives.

The four men had been in this conversation a good part of the night. They were hungry and sat on the ground around the *shulhan* (a low table) made of leather and spread on the ground. Three *menorahs* (lamps) maintained some light in the small room.

The host and his wife brought the olives and bread they would be eating while drinking some wine. The two apostles asked the Levite about his family back home and the olive business in Cyprus. Besides this business his father had also left him two properties that produced excellent grapes from which the locals made a delicious wine. The grapes were sold locally but the olives were sold mostly in Antioch and also in Jerusalem and Judea.

John mentioned that he and his brother James had left the fishing business in good shape and entrusted it to three of their faithful employees. Peter had sold his fishing business to a friend and was spending most of his time in Jerusalem with the other apostles working with the Church.

The four men continued to talked a good part of the night. Barnabas had only one day left in Jerusalem before returning to Cyprus. The Levite had more questions about the resurrection and the events that followed.

He was eager to ask Peter and John about what happened after the death of Jesus and how these men and so many others came to believe that he had come back to life after his crucifixion. The conversation continued after their light meal.

7. WITNESSES

Turning to John, Barnabas asked: "How did you and the other apostles discover that Jesus had risen from the dead?" And Barnabas added: "Since Jesus had mentioned this a number of times during his ministry to you and the other apostles, you all must have been eager to see the Master at his resurrection."

To his surprise John responded saying, "Joseph, none of us had understood that Jesus had in fact prophesied of his resurrection from the dead after his cruel death. After his death on the cross, our hearts were heavy and full of anxiety. We asked ourselves what would happen now? Should we return to Galilee and get back with our families, our friends? The Master had been crucified and had died on the day preceding the Sabbath and none of us could travel or do much during the day of rest. We all knew that we would need to decide something concerning our future as soon as the Sabbath day was over. Our Lord had done such amazing signs that nobody else had ever done, had taught us for three years and was now dead like any other human being."

"Yes", continued Peter, "John is correct. The eleven of us apostles and some of the women who had followed Jesus were like sheep left without a shepherd."

"What happened then?" asked the Levite.

Peter spoke these words: "Very early on the day following the Sabbath, after an entire night of waiting and worrying, and while it was still dark outside, we heard loud knocking on the door of the small house where we had gathered. It was Matthew who went and opened the door and saw Mary of Magdala who nearly shouted at us, 'They have taken the Lord's body out of the tomb, and we don't know where they have put him!" (John 20.2)."

Peter continued: "John and I we rose up and started running to the rock-cut tomb of Joseph of Arimathea. John got there before me but did not enter the tomb. I reached the tomb right after him and what I saw was hard to believe. The body of the Lord was gone. The linen wrappings he had been buried with were still lying on the slab, but the body was gone. The cloth that covered his head was folded and lying apart from the wrappings."

Joseph thought, *so the body of Jesus had been treated with the greatest care for his buria*l. This was something which was only done for the rich of the land. He knew that the bodies of those crucified were left by the Romans on the crosses to rot and to be devoured by birds. Families were not allowed to take the bodies down from these crosses. When the bones fell from the crosses they were thrown in the river or in the garbage.

Joseph recalled the importance of linen wrappings for burials. He said to Peter, "So Jesus' body was treated with the greatest care for his burial?"

The apostle responded: "Joseph of Arimathea and his friend Nicodemus were given permission by Pilate to take down the body of Jesus from the cross on the day of his death which was Friday, the day of preparation for the Sabbath. They came with the mixture of aloe and myrrh, took the body down from the cross and bound the body in linen cloths as is the custom. They then laid the body in the tomb of Joseph," responded Peter.

Barnabas asked, "So the body was bound tightly with swaths of cloths or bandages as is our custom?"

"Precisely!" responded John, "Joseph and Nicodemus took great care of Jesus' body as they would for a family member."

These words were followed by a rather long silence in the room. Barnabas was thinking. *There was no way the body of Jesus could have been unwrapped from the tight bandages covering his entire body.* The body had just vanished out of the bandages.

As he was thinking about this, the Levite also remembered the words of the prophet Isaiah concerning the suffering Messiah, "They made his grave with the wicked and with the rich in his death". (Isaiah 53.9).

Despite being very tired after an entire night of discussion, Barnabas continued the conversation and asked more questions to Peter and John.

He learned that the women, Mary of Magdala, Mary the mother of James and Salome had come to the tomb very early on the first day of the week with more spices and wondered how the heavy and large stone would be rolled over for them to enter the rock-cut tomb. When they arrived, the tomb was already opened. In the tomb someone was sitting on the right side of the slab and wearing white clothes. The women were very fearful of this presence in the tomb. But with great calm, a young person in white began speaking to them, "Don't be alarmed. You are looking for Jesus of Nazareth, who was crucified. He isn't here! He is risen from the dead! Look, this is where they laid his body. [7] Now go and tell his disciples, including Peter, that Jesus is going ahead of you to Galilee. You will see him there, just as he told you before he died.". (Mark 16.6-8).

The story of Jesus did not end with this account of what happened to the women at the tomb and how Peter and John first ran to the tomb and saw it was empty. The Lord also instructed his disciples to go to Galilee where they would again see him.

The guards who had been guarding the tomb had fled at the sudden appearing of the angel white as snow, powerful as lightening striking the earth. Some of them went to the chief priests and told them what had happened. The chief priests and elders met together and decided to give a substantial amount of money to these guards and instructed them to tell everyone that the body of Jesus had been stolen while they were sleeping.

John and Peter continued to talk about the times Jesus appeared to them and the other apostles for a period of forty days, first in Jerusalem and also in Galilee. As he had done during his three years of teaching, Jesus had taught them many things concerning the Kingdom of God and the mission they were to fulfill of preaching the Gospel of salvation to all the nations, starting in Jerusalem.

During these forty days, the resurrected Jesus instructed his apostles concerning the Law, the prophets and the Psalms. They all pointed to the Messiah who would suffer and on the third day rise from the dead; repentance and forgiveness of sins would be preached to all the nations, beginning with Jerusalem.

The words of the prophet Isaiah came to mind as the Levite thought of so many of the Scriptures that taught Israel to expect God's blessings extended to all nations:

> "Arise, Jerusalem! Let your light shine for all to see.
>   For the glory of the LORD rises to shine on you.
> ² Darkness as black as night covers all the nations of

the earth,
　　but the glory of the Lord rises and appears over you.
³ All nations will come to your light;
　　mighty kings will come to see your radiance."
(Isaiah 60.1-3)

Exhausted, Barnabas breathed deeply. His entire life, his identity as an Israelite and a Levite seemed to be in question. *If death had truly been conquered through Jesus, this meant that God had entered this world in a powerful and unique way.*

The sun had already risen. It was time to end this meeting. The four men had spent the entire night and part of the day in conversation. They sat in silence for some time as if to let these words sink deep into the heart of each one.

Barnabas was now thinking about his wife Sarah and his two boys. A plan was being formed in his mind. He would soon return to Cyprus and share all of this with his family. As he thought about this, Barnabas decided that he was going to ask Mark to accompany him to Cyprus.

The Lord had blessed Barnabas with property and means and his plan was to return as soon as possible to Jerusalem and bring his family along so they too could meet with Peter and John and the other disciples in Jerusalem. He would need to settle in Jerusalem for some time and learn from these men and other disciples like his cousin Mark and his mother.

What he had heard was amazing news. The entire world would be changed by what Jesus did and by his victory over death. Barnabas could not wait to talk about all of this to his family.

The three men prayed together and sang Psalms for some time. Finally, Peter and John rose up, embraced Barnabas and left the house.

8. CYPRUS

Two days later, Mark and Barnabas left for Cyprus.

The plan was clear. Barnabas would need to move his family to Jerusalem. This would not be a source of great anxiety for Sarah since she, like myself, had uncles, aunts as well as cousins in the city of David. It would be more difficult for the boys who had many friends who attended our synagogue.

The business was prosperous, and Barnabas knew he could count on Eliezer, himself a Benjamite, to take care of everything. Eliezer was such a wonderful helper and deserved the name he had been given and which means "help of my God". He and Barnabas had grown up together and were of the same age. Barnabas felt blessed to have him as steward of his lands and business, a brother Israelite in whom he had complete trust, a man devoted to the God of Israel and to the local Synagogue.

Mark and Barnabas left Jerusalem early in the morning and first traveled partly by foot and cart to the port of *Sykaminos* on the Great Sea — a port and fishing town that had been given its Greek name sycamore and was close to the slopes of Mount Carmel. The sycamore was the tree Jesus had mentioned when he taught his disciples, saying "If you had faith even as small as a mustard seed, you could say to this mulberry (sycamore) tree, 'May you be uprooted and be planted in the sea,' and it would obey you!" (Luke 17.6). The tree provides food both for humans and animals. Birds are known to eat its leaves and fruit which tastes somewhat like the fig. The sycamore is also a symbol of renewal and return to God. Zacchaeus was sitting on a sycamore tree when Jesus called him, and he became a disciple (Luke 19.1-10).

From *Sykaminos* our ship sailed on the Great Sea towards *Limassol*, an ancient port of Cyprus between the towns of *Amathus* and *Kourion* on the southern coast of the island. The ship was similar to the one the apostle Paul embarked on when he traveled to Rome. (Acts 27). It was rather large and could carry over 200 people. A great part of the space on the ship was for carrying grain and other goods and travelers had little room to move. Strong winds usually blew on the southern side of Cyprus, so after many hours of sailing on the Great Sea, one could be ill from the winds and waves tossing the ship up and down for hours.

Barnabas dreaded the last part of sailing to *Limassol*, but this time the winds were mild and the sea calmer than usual. Along with Mark, he thanked God and both were relieved to set foot back on the land.

From *Limassol* to his home, Barnabas and Mark traveled towards *Salamis* on the eastern part of the Island. Salamis is part of the Roman province of Cilicia which had been annexed to the Roman republic by Pompey. The town of Tarsus, where brother Paul was born, was also in the roman province of Cilicia. Both Paul and Barnabas, being born in a Roman province, had Roman citizenship as well as being Israelites. Later this made it easier for Barnabas to travel to Tarsus and find Paul in order to bring him to Jerusalem.

Mark and Barnabas reached *Salamis* two days later, very tired by the miles of walking and cart riding on rough and at times bumpy roads.

All along this voyage Barnabas did not cease to pray about how he would share the news about Jesus with his wife and boys. He prayed constantly to God that we would find the words to touch their hearts and help them understand why our family needed to move for a time to the city of David.

Thankfully, the two men reached their destination when it was not yet dark. Traveling by foot, cart or ship never guaranteed safe travels. Both Mark and Barnabas entrusted their days on the roads and sea to God, reminding each other of some of the Psalms sung by the pilgrims on their way to worship the Lord:

> [1] I look up to the mountains—
>   does my help come from there?
> [2] My help comes from the LORD,
>   who made heaven and earth!
> [3] He will not let you stumble;
>   the one who watches over you will not slumber.
> [4] Indeed, he who watches over Israel
>   never slumbers or sleeps.
> [5] The LORD himself watches over you!
>   The LORD stands beside you as your protective shade.
> [6] The sun will not harm you by day,
>   nor the moon at night.
> [7] The LORD keeps you from all harm
>   and watches over your life.
> [8] The LORD keeps watch over you as you come and go,
>   both now and forever.
> (Psalms 121)

Just as the sun was setting down on the Great Sea, Sarah and the boys heard the cart from far away and ran out of the house to greet the two men. Eliezer, his wife Esther, as well as five-year-old son Jonathan, were also present to greet the men.

It was wonderful for all of them to be together once more. The boys were greatly excited about Mark's presence. Everyone was anxious to get news from uncles and aunts and many cousins. That evening they had an amazing meal of lamb and a stew of vegetables.

Barnabas offered the traditional night blessing as the young people went to bed. The adults continued talking well into the night. Barnabas described his few weeks in Jerusalem and his encounter with the believers in Jesus of Nazareth and all that the apostles Peter and John had shared with him.

Sarah was eager to hear more about all of this. Eliezer and Esther seemed more guarded about the story of Jesus and the testimony of the apostles. They listened however with interest to Mark, who had known and seen the Master personally, and been close to the fishermen Peter and John.

Eliezer had been brought up in the smallest tribe of Israel, Benjamin, which had some of the greatest heroes of God's people such as the judge Ehud as well as Mordecai and Esther who delivered the people from certain death under the rule of the Persian kings. (Esther 2.5-7).

That evening Barnabas and Eliezer discussed the business arrangements for the months to come, especially the picking of the olives and those who would be hired to make the olive oil and have it ready for shipment. Eliezer would be in charge of everything, and would keep communicating with his master during his absence. The two men agreed that the family would leave the day following the sabbath thus in five days.

9. JERUSALEM

Their travel to Jerusalem lasted eight days. The group lost three entire days at Limassol waiting for a ship to sail. The winds being so strong that no ship could venture on the Sea. After this delay they finally got on a ship and reached the coast safely. It was early in December.

It took Mark and the family two more days to reach Jerusalem, traveling in company of an important group of pilgrims heading to Jerusalem for the feast of *Hanukah* ("the festival of lights" or "feast of dedication"), eight days of celebration going back to the time of the Maccabees when the temple was cleansed and rededicated after the period of desecration caused by pagan ruler Antiochus IV Epiphanes.

During *Hanukah,* each household places the *Hanukah lamp* outside the entrance of the house. There is a recitation of the entire Hallel (Psalms 113-118) on each of the eight days. Israelites also read from the *Torah* (the Law of Moses) about the kindling of the Menorah. (Numbers 7.1-8.4).

The shortest of the Psalms is found among the Hallel:

> [1] Praise the LORD, all you nations.
>> Praise him, all you people of the earth.
> [2] For his unfailing love for us is powerful;
>> the LORD's faithfulness endures forever.
> Praise the LORD!
> (Psalm 117.1,2)

It was during *Hanukkah* that Jesus taught in the temple about the Good Shepherd, "[22] It was now winter, and Jesus was in Jerusalem at the time of Hanukkah, the Festival of Dedication. [23] He was in the Temple, walking through the section known as Solomon's Colonnade. [24] The people surrounded him and asked, 'How long are you going to keep us in suspense? If you are the Messiah, tell us plainly.'" (John 10.22-24).

John in his Gospel describes Jesus at the very beginning of his teaching ministry entering the temple and "cleansing it" as is also prophesied in the Scriptures: "[13] It was nearly time for the Jewish Passover celebration, so Jesus went to Jerusalem. [14] In the Temple area he saw merchants selling cattle, sheep, and doves for sacrifices; he also saw dealers at tables exchanging foreign money. [15] Jesus made a whip from some ropes and chased them all out of the Temple. He drove out the sheep and cattle, scattered the money changers' coins over the floor, and turned over their tables. [16] Then, going over to the people who sold doves, he told them, "Get these things out of here. Stop turning my Father's house into a marketplace!" [17] Then his disciples remembered this prophecy from the Scriptures: 'Passion for God's house will consume me.'" (John 2.13-17; Psalm 69.9).

For over six months now, Barnabas had been hearing about the events first mentioned by his Uncle Ben and later described by Mark and finally by the apostles, the witnesses of Jesus' life and of his teachings, his death and resurrection.

The Levite had been searching and meditating the Scriptures more than ever, especially the Psalms and Isaiah the prophet.

As Joseph watched his family during their travel to Jerusalem, he did not sense any anxiety in their words or behavior. The day they had left Cyprus it had been difficult to say good-by to friends and neighbors. As they traveled and the days went by,

Joseph sensed the excitement of everyone in the prospect of meeting family members they had not seen for many years or others they had never met.

As they approached Jerusalem, the weather got much colder and they were all eager to reach their new house and find warmth and food. Several miles away as they looked up to Mount Zion, they could see the many lights of *Hannukah* flickering at the start of the night.

It was a beautiful sight which always warmed the hearts of pilgrims who traveled sometimes from very far away to the city of David. Joseph thought *all these lights represent each home, each man, woman and child and each one needs light to go about at night, each one struggles with the dark forces of evil and sin.*

Statements from the Hallel Psalms came to his mind (they are the Psalms read and sung at Hanukah):

> "⁶ The LORD is for me, so I will have no fear.
>   What can mere people do to me?
> ⁷ Yes, the LORD is for me; he will help me.
>   I will look in triumph at those who hate me.
> ⁸ It is better to take refuge in the LORD
>   than to trust in people.
> ⁹ It is better to take refuge in the LORD
>   than to trust in princes."
> (Psalm 118.7-9)

This Psalm also mentioned the stone rejected by the builders of God's house but which became the cornerstone. *Who was the stone? David or one of the prophets? If David, how could this be since the king had sinned against God?* Barnabas wondered if the cornerstone could be the people of Israel rejected by Gentiles, as some of the teachers of Israel believed and taught.

Barnabas also remembered that Isaiah the prophet mentions the cornerstone, "a firm and tested stone" rejected by the builders or leaders of the people. This message was given to Isaiah at a time when the prophet was warning the leaders of our divided people, Israel and Judah who had fallen into sin and rebellion against God and who were no different from the rulers of pagan nations:

> "¹⁶ Therefore, this is what the Sovereign LORD says:
> 'Look! I am placing a foundation stone in Jerusalem,
>   a firm and tested stone.
> It is a precious cornerstone that is safe to build on.
>   Whoever believes need never be shaken.'"
> (Isaiah 28.16)

The group finally reached the city of David.

They were approaching the pool of Siloam using the large road which had been built by Pilate for the many pilgrims and visitors to enter the city. It was from the pool of Siloam that pilgrims would start their ascent to the Temple mount that led to the Temple court. The pool was fed by the waters of the *Gihon Spring*. The pool of Siloam was a giant *mikveh* (ritual bath) where the pilgrims would purify themselves before heading to the Temple Court with their offerings.

They walked for about half a mile on the large pilgrim road leading to the Temple area. During day time, thousands of pilgrims crowded the road filled with stalls and merchants on each side. Merchants paid a hefty tax to be able to sell their goods in one of those stalls. But now it was late at night on the *day of preparation* (Friday or the day before the Sabbath). Only a few dogs were going about scavenging for food and small groups of soldiers were posted here and there, protecting the homes of some of the Roman and Jewish authorities of the city.

They finally came close to the *Royal Stoa* (Royal Porch) where the *Sanhedrin* (the ruling court) met.

Exhausted by days of traveling, they first headed to Mark's house closer to the upper city, west of the Temple area where the priestly families lived as well as the ruling class. They were also coming closer to the *Antonia Fortress* built by Herod on the Northwest Side of the Temple area.

They finally reached Mark's home — a large two-story stone construction. The house Barnabas had purchased close to his cousin's home was modest when compared to the white marble mansions of some of the religious rulers and priestly families living in that area of Jerusalem. However, this house would be ideal for their small family and well located for shopping and visiting other family members. Joseph was not certain how long they would live in Jerusalem before returning to Cyprus. He chose to purchase a house that could be sold easily if needed because of its location.

They were all warmly greeted by Mark's mother, by uncle Ben and his wife Esther. They all had waited for the group to arrive before sharing a late meal. They sat on the carpets covering the floor, so glad to have reached their destination safely and in good health. They ate a delicious stew and bread that had been baked in an oven heated by twigs placed on several hot stones covered with coals.

The day ended with a blessing by uncle Ben, and the singing of the Hallel Psalm which ends with these words of blessing:

"²⁶ Bless the one who comes in the name of the Lᴏʀᴅ.

We bless you from the house of the Lᴏʀᴅ.

²⁷ The Lᴏʀᴅ is God, shining upon us.

Take the sacrifice and bind it with cords on the altar.

²⁸ You are my God, and I will praise you!

You are my God, and I will exalt you!

²⁹ Give thanks to the Lᴏʀᴅ, for he is good!

His faithful love endures forever."

(Psalm 118.26-29)

1.

10. PETER, JOHN AND JAMES

Joseph and his family, as well as Mark, reached Jerusalem on a Friday (also called day of preparation or *Shishi*). The next day would be Sabbath and they would attend the local synagogue and rest from their travels. Arriving in Jerusalem later than planned, they had missed a good part of the gatherings and rejoicings at the synagogue and also the temple.

That year the last day of the feast of *Hannukah* fell on *Rishon,* the day following the Sabbath (the first day of the week, Sunday). On that day all the eight lights were glowing in each household.

The book of Genesis taught that God created everything in six days and rested on the seventh day, the Sabbath. The day following Sabbath was thus an "eighth day"- a day of new beginnings, a day representing the hope that comes from God's faithful word of promise. It was also on the eighth day that the male child was circumcised as a sign of the covenant between Abraham and God. In the book of Exodus, the tabernacle was completed on the first of Nisan (Exodus 40) and consecrated eight days later (Leviticus 9).

The plan was to meet with Peter, John and James at the home of one of Jesus' disciples in the lower part of the city.

Joseph, Sarah, their sons Elijah and Samuel arrived for lunch at the humble home of this family of five who were also followers of Jesus. The main room was full, with sixteen gathered to hear the apostles, including Mark and his mother as well as Ben and his wife Esther.

The couple had heard about the apostles but had never met these men. Joseph had prepared his family for this meeting by telling them everything he had learned from Mark. Ben had been in conversation with Mark and his mother for over a year concerning Jesus and his teachings as well as the accounts of his death and resurrection.

The main room of the humble dwelling had a small stove guests could gather around, since it was cold outside. There was a bed in one corner as well as a hand-mill. This was a very basic shelter, almost like a tent when compared to the luxurious homes built on the higher side of the city close to the Temple grounds.

But it was a place of refuge from the cold and sometimes dangers of the outside world.

The poor of the land would understand deeply the words of the Psalms describing God as the true and lasting shelter:

> "¹ O God, listen to my cry!
>   Hear my prayer!
> ² From the ends of the earth,
>   I cry to you for help
>   when my heart is overwhelmed.
> Lead me to the towering rock of safety,
> ³   for you are my safe refuge,
>   a fortress where my enemies cannot reach me.
> ⁴ Let me live forever in your sanctuary,
>   safe beneath the shelter of your wings!"
> (Psalms 61.1-4)

They all huddled close to the stove. Everyone was already there when Peter, James and his brother John entered the house, away from the bitter cold. There was nothing about the appearance or clothes worn by these men that indicated any special social or religious status. However, a mysterious solemnity and dignity, as well as joy radiated from these three men, even though they had not yet uttered one word. Everyone had enjoyed the lights of Hannukah and its celebrations but in the presence of Peter, John and James, Joseph felt another kind of light difficult to describe but which reached down to the very core of his being, down to his soul.

After the meal, Peter, James, John and even Mark shared the story of Jesus from his birth to his ascension. This account took several hours, well into the afternoon. Even the two sons of Joseph, as well as the three younger children of their host family seemed completely captivated by the events of the life of Jesus.

No one said a word or interrupted this amazing account.

Jesus of Nazareth spoke with a unique authority stemming from his own person. One statement made a strong impression on the Levite: "I tell you the truth, those who listen to my message and believe in God who sent me have eternal life. They will never be condemned for their sins, but they have already passed from death into life." (John 5.24).

The apostle Peter ended the account of Jesus' life with the words he and the apostles had heard in Galilee after his resurrection, "I have been given all authority in heaven and on earth. [19] Therefore, go and make disciples of all the nations, baptizing them in the name of the Father and the Son and the Holy Spirit. [20] Teach these new disciples to obey all the commands I have given you. And be sure of this: I am with you always, even to the end of the age." (Matthew 28.16-20)

When Peter finished speaking, they all remained silent for what seemed a very long time.

Barnabas was thinking, *Can an Israelite follow Jesus as Messiah and still be part of Israel? Would he need to abandon and turn away from his loved ones, his friends and family?*

As if knowing what troubled him, John broke the silence and spoke the following words to Barnabas: "We are to be the light and the salt to our people and even to the world. How can one be the light somewhere if he is not present, if he is absent from a place? Jesus prayed fervently before the cross and said in his prayer, '15 I'm not asking you to take them out of the world, but to keep them safe from the evil one. 16 They do not belong to this world any more than I do. 17 Make them holy by your truth; teach them your word, which is truth.'" (John 17.16,17).

Barnabas was also troubled by the thought of how Jesus had been treated by those in the higher positions of authority. James had mentioned in his speech how following the Master would bring about even hatred and rejection in this world. The Hannukah feast of the past week had just reminded the Levite and his family of how the pagan king Antiochus had treated their people, had killed many and desecrated the temple.

Barnabas spoke up and said to the three apostles: "Mark told us how thousands among our people, not long ago, were immersed in the name of Jesus on the day of Pentecost and even later. Is this something Jesus is asking us to do? What is God asking us to do so we can enjoy forgiveness of sins and to enter into the new covenant?"

John responded with these words: "The Lord is asking everyone to believe in him with all their heart and to turn away from sin. This is all one needs to do to enter this covenant of forgiveness and in order to receive His gift of the Holy Spirit.

Yes, on the day of Pentecost many came to faith in Jesus and were immersed into his name for the remission of sins and the gift of the Holy Spirit."

"John" replied Barnabas "Is this what is meant by the teachings of Jesus concerning the birth from water and the Spirit which you mentioned earlier in the discussion with Nicodemus, the doctor of the law?"

John responded with these words, "Joseph, when Jesus taught about the birth from above, the new birth, he was talking about a birth that has its origin in God, a birth that gives access to the Kingdom of God. The Kingdom of God has come to us in the person of the Messiah. Remember Joseph, the Messiah is the king, the offspring of David, the ruler of God's people in accordance with the promises made by God to David. (2 Samuel chapter 7). This is about people coming under the rule of the anointed one, the one who leads us to God's Kingdom which is an eternal kingdom as promised to David, "Your house and your kingdom shall be made sure forever before me".

Hearing these words from John, the Levite thought about the covenant God had made with king David and his offspring. Jesus of Nazareth had died with the words written on the cross in Hebrew, Greek and Latin, "Jesus the Nazarene, king of the Jews". He also remembered the account of Mark about John the Baptist, "all the country of Judea and all Jerusalem were going out to him and were being baptized by him in the river Jordan, confessing their sins," (Mark 1.5). Was there a connection between the kingship of David and the Jordan river?"

The apostle John spoke again, as if knowing the thoughts of the Levite: "The river Jordan does not have the power to purify anyone from their sins. Only God has that power and only through his sacrificial lamb as John proclaimed when he saw Jesus 'Behold, the lamb of God.'"

Joseph knew that many, like himself, descended from Levi and some from the high priesthood, but it had been a rare occasion for him to offer an animal sacrifice in the temple. He also knew that the Levitical priests of ancient Israel were required to be without physical defect and ritually pure before performing their duties. The book of Leviticus outlined the requirements for the purity that God required of priests. A descendant of Aaron had to be pure, unspotted and without physical defects before he could offer sacrifices or any offering to God.

Having thought about this, Joseph spoke to the three apostles: "Are we to understand that this is the start of a new priesthood, since we are talking about a new covenant, the one promised by prophets like Jeremiah? Are you, apostles, now these priests of God who offer sacrifices?"

Peter answered and said, "Joseph, the priesthood in the new covenant is extended to all who enter this covenant. All who come through Jesus to God enter his "house", his "temple" to serve him through their entire lives and to offer themselves as priests of God. As the priests purified themselves, so the followers of the Messiah need to purify themselves and receive remission of sins. On Pentecost when the people asked us what they need to do, this is the answers we gave them from the Lord: "Each of you must repent of your sins and turn to God and be baptized in the name of Jesus Christ for the forgiveness of your sins. Then you will receive the gift of the Holy Spirit. [39] This promise is to you, to your children, and to those far away — all who have been called by the Lord our God." (Acts 2.38,39).

"Those who follow the Christ and serve him are in God's sight a royal priesthood, God's own special people", added Peter.

This conversation lasted well into the late afternoon. Joseph and his family, as well as Ben and Esther, were deeply touched by the witness of these men and how the Scriptures confirmed the claims and work of Jesus of Nazareth.

11. BAPTISMS

After the apostles had finished speaking, they all left the house and walked together towards the upper city. Joseph and Mark went by their homes to take covers since the weather was cold and baptism in the pools of Siloam would prove difficult at this time of the year. The two houses were only ten minutes away from the very large pools adjoining the Temple.

At the pool, the apostles asked Mark to baptize Joseph, Sarah and the two boys in the pool. Ben and his wife Esther were present but were not baptized at that time. They would be baptized months later, at the same time many of the priests came to faith in Jesus as Messiah. (Acts 6.7)

Barnabas wondered why Peter, John or James did not baptize him or his family. He understood later especially traveling with Paul in his missionary journeys that the importance and meaning of baptism were not in the water itself, the place of baptism or even the person performing the baptism, but in the faith and sincere repentance of the believer and God's action of forgiveness towards those who repent. The apostle Paul even wrote to the Christians in Corinth the following words: "Were any of you baptized in the name of Paul? Of course not! [14] I thank God that I did not baptize any of you except Crispus and Gaius, [15] for now no one can say they were baptized in my name. [16] (Oh yes, I also baptized the household of Stephanas, but I don't remember baptizing anyone else.) [17] For Christ didn't send me to baptize, but to preach the Good News—and not with clever speech, for fear that the cross of Christ would lose its power." (1 Corinthians 1.13-17).

Another important matter Joseph understood was that having come to faith in Jesus as the promised Messiah did not mean he needed to abandon his people or even their customs. It meant, as John had mentioned, that through Jesus, his disciples were called to live as light and salt among the people and in the world.

Thus, began for Joseph and his family, a new life among his people and among those who live in darkness in the Gentile world.

As Paul later wrote to Timothy, God came and lived as a servant in the flesh in order that he might save all peoples from their sins and bring them into his family, his household, the "church of the living God": "14 I hope to come to you soon, but I am writing these things to you so that, 15 if I delay, you may know how one ought to behave in the household of God, which is the church of the living God, a pillar and buttress of the truth. 16 Great indeed, we confess, is the mystery of godliness:

> He was manifested in the flesh,
> vindicated by the Spirit,
> seen by angels,
> proclaimed among the nations,
> believed on in the world,
> taken up in glory."
> (1 Timothy 3.14-16, ESV)

At the time of their baptism, Tiberius was still the emperor in Rome. The Roman legions were still present in Jerusalem and throughout much of the world. The Jewish people were still paying heavy taxes to cruel rulers. From the perspective of earth and the material world, it seemed that nothing had changed.

What Barnabas had come to believe was that the power of Jesus' sacrificial work on the cross and the power of his reign in human hearts, was bringing complete change in the lives of those who believed and obeyed the Lord, who returned to God in humility and repentance.

At about the time when Barnabas and his family came to faith, the number of men who had believed in Christ in Jerusalem was about five thousand. The Sadducees, who teach that there is no resurrection or even angels or demons, had put Peter and John under arrest and had forbidden them to preach in the name of Jesus. (Acts 4.1-4).

Many wonders and signs were being done through the apostles of Jesus. Such was the healing of the crippled man. Peter spoke to the rulers about this healing, saying: "Rulers and elders of our people, [9] are we being questioned today because we've done a good deed for a crippled man? Do you want to know how he was healed? [10] Let me clearly state to all of you and to all the people of Israel that he was healed by the powerful name of Jesus Christ the Nazarene, the man you crucified but whom God raised from the dead." (Acts 4.9,10)

Thousands of Jewish pilgrims had come to faith in Jesus during Pentecost two years before. Many more had heard the Gospel and had come to faith in Jesus. Many of these followers of Jesus had remained in Jerusalem, meeting daily at the temple, receiving instruction from the apostles.

It was at this time that many who had wealth sold belongings or property to help feed all of those who had no means to buy food or even to find lodging. Barnabas sent an emissary to Cyprus asking Eliezer to sell a field that produced grapes close to his farm and to have the money brought to Jerusalem. Many others who owned lands or houses sold them that year and brought needed relief to those in need. (Acts 4.35-37).

From that time on, the apostles called Joseph by the name Barnabas, which means "Son of encouragement". In his book of Acts, the writer Luke also describes him as a "man filled with the Holy Spirit and faith" (Acts 11.24). This meant that Joseph the Levite, was known as a caring man. He cared for the welfare of those around him. Barnabas was known to find the time to be concerned about others — about their welfare, their spiritual growth. He was known as a great encourager to everyone he met.

Barnabas cared for others and was an encourager even when it put him in trouble and cost him a lot. He extended his love and warmth to Saul of Tarsus when Jerusalem was still very afraid of the apostle and would not welcome him. Barnabas came forward as the encourager to Paul and showed great kindness toward him. He took great pains to introduce him to the apostles.

12.   SAUL OF TARSUS

A little over three years had passed since Barnabas moved to Jerusalem with his family. His life had been completely turned around with the knowledge of the Gospel and meeting the witnesses of Jesus' life.

He had met Peter and James on a few occasions. He was now a little over forty years old, just a few years older than Jesus' apostles. Stephen's stoning was known throughout Jerusalem and the land. Those who stoned this Christian who was a deacon in the Church, were of the Synagogue of the "Freedmen", a synagogue mainly composed of Gentile proselytes from Alexandria and the region of Cilicia. (Acts 6.8-15).

The proselytes to Judaism from the Gentile world were very zealous for the law, sometimes more than Pharisees, as Jesus himself had mentioned (Matthew 23.15). At that time, a young man by the name of Saul, himself a Pharisee, who was one of the most promising students of Gamaliel, had approved the stoning of Stephen and had obtained letters from the religious authorities to travel land and sea to arrest, imprison and even kill the followers of Jesus.

Paul was from Cilicia, a Roman region. Cyprus had also been made part of Cilicia by the Roman authorities. Like Barnabas, Paul was Jewish but was also a Roman citizen.

After his encounter with the risen Christ on the road to Damascus, Saul came briefly to Jerusalem. He started attending the Synagogue and was asked to comment on the readings from the Scriptures. He began teaching about the Lord Jesus and proclaim the Good News of salvation in His name.

He quickly faced intense opposition especially from the proselytes of Judaism who came from the Greek world (they were called the Hellenists). Some witnessed the debates between Paul and the Hellenists and spread the news about what was happening in Jerusalem with the former persecutor of Christians.

This is how Barnabas heard about Paul and the fact that this new Christian was in danger. He understood that this brother needed help as well as encouragement. He believed that it would be important for Paul to meet with the apostles.

As Barnabas inquired about Paul, he learned that he was a tent maker. He knew the main tent makers in Jerusalem and was determined, if possible, to find Paul among them.

Throughout the Roman empire, artisans flocked to the main cities to set up shop or work with others. The average shop where tents are made of goat leather would have about ten to twelve slaves and sometimes freedmen working together. The shops had a door wide opened or a window open to the street. The owners of those shops lived upstairs, while the workers, some of them only passing through town, slept on cots during the night. Like many other workers, most of these artisans were often hired for a few days at a time.

Barnabas shared with no one except Sarah his plan to go and look for Paul. After they both prayed and asked for guidance and protection in seeking the apostle, Barnabas left his house early one morning.

Barnabas knew where to go. The Jerusalem marketplace occupied mainly one street running from the higher part of the city where the wealthy had their houses and where the temple stood to the downtown and poor areas of the city. Along this street there were at that time three major stores with tent makers.

The first shop Barnabas went to belonged to a man by the name of David, son of Jonas. The weather was bitter cold, so the market was not very busy that day. However, the main door stood open in case potential clients passed by. The Son of encouragement pushed open the door of David's shop, which also had two large windows viewing the street, allowing for light, as tent makers worked inside.

Barnabas spoke out loud, saying "David, my brother, are you here?" Five men were all working together on one large piece of leather extending over two tables. Barnabas immediately recognized his friend David who was watching over the entire process and turned to him with a big smile and exclaimed, "Joseph my brother, what a surprise!"

The head tent maker gave instructions to the four other workers and led Barnabas upstairs to meet to talk and have some food with wine. He took a jar of olives from a shelf at the back of the room and held it proudly, saying: "Joseph, I want you to taste the best olives in all of the world." Of course, David was praising olives which he had bought directly from Joseph.

The two friends talked for a while about the business and family matters. The tent maker had two grown up sons, Andrew and Caleb. They had also learned the tent-making trade but had recently moved to the city of Antioch to start a shop together.

"David, asked Barnabas, I am looking for a tent-maker from Tarsus whose name is Saul. He has recently come to Jerusalem and I need to meet with him."

David replied: "Joseph, I have not met this man Saul. For the past few years, I have tried not to hire workers for a day or a few days. I have only four tent makers, but I prefer to have them with me for longer periods of time."

David added, "If you go up closer to the temple, you can talk with Jonathan who uses mostly daily workers and has usually about fifteen tent makers with him. It is the largest shop in the city, and he might be able to help you."

After the usual greetings and blessings, Barnabas left David's shop and walked up the market street for about twenty minutes until he saw on his right a shop somewhat larger than most others. It was bitter cold but here also the door was open, with two large windows on each side that could be opened in good weather for selling the tents. The freedmen or slaves who made the tents were also those who would be selling the tents along with the shop owner when crowds would be walking up and down the street.

A tall man with broad shoulders and a stern demeanor was standing at the door to keep intruders from walking in but also ready to address potential buyers. Barnabas was rather tall himself, but this man was clearly taller than most men.

When Jonathan saw Barnabas approaching him, he immediately started praising the high quality of his goat-hair and leather tents and the amazing price he was selling them for. As a good salesman, he invited Barnabas to a small shop nearby for a drink and some food so they could talk. He was certain Barnabas was one of those wealthy Jews from abroad who had moved recently to Jerusalem or was doing business in Jerusalem.

Jonathan was clearly disappointed when Barnabas told him that David had given him his information and that he was looking for a tent maker named Saul of Tarsus.

After Barnabas mentioned the name of Saul, Jonathan remained silent for a moment and said, "Saul must be the freedman I hired three days ago. He is an amazing worker and highly educated. I asked him a few questions before hiring him for a couple of days. I learned to my surprise that he had been one of the outstanding students of Gamaliel, the famous Torah teacher."

Taking a sip from his brew Jonathan added: "I did hesitate at first because I am somewhat weary of scholars who speak a lot but are not able to do much more. But when I saw the ability of this man Saul as a tent maker, I decided to hire him."

Barnabas was greatly encouraged by these words and asked Jonathan, "How is Saul as a tent maker?"

"I am very pleased with his work" responded the tent maker. "At first, when I asked him a few questions about the trade, especially the quality of leather and even where to buy it and how to get it prepared, I immediately recognized a highly capable tent maker. Saul stays here at night and sleeps on a cot at the back of the shop. The first night be stayed here I invited him upstairs to speak to our family about the Torah. I have heard some of our famous rabbis speak and teach but this man seems to surpass them all in knowledge and can answer any question we have concerning the Tora and even the prophets. I don't think in my entire life I have spent so much time with one teacher talking about religion."

Barnabas and Jonathan started walking back to the shop and entered through the door, enjoying the warmth after bitter cold weather.

Jonathan had described the kind of man Saul was and Barnabas immediately recognized him as soon as he entered the shop.

He was joining together two sides of a large tent but bending more than the other workers. Apparently, he was not able to see very well. But as mentioned by Jonathan, he seemed very skilled at what he was doing.

As the two men entered the shop and watched Paul, he did not at first appear distracted from his task. This was a man completely focused on what he was doing.

After a moment, Saul suddenly realized the presence of Barnabas and Jonathan and turning around gave both men a friendly and welcoming look. There was a peace and a joy on his face and in his eyes that Barnabas recognized immediately. It was the same impression he had seen on the faces of Peter and from James and John.

As Saul looked into the eyes of Barnabas, he seemed to know immediately that this man was a follower of the Master. An immense sense of relief and joy immediately came upon Saul's face.

"Brother Paul", said Barnabas, "I will need to leave now but I need to ask you to come with me tomorrow to meet with other disciples." Barnabas had already agreed with Jonathan that he would ask his worker to accompany him at least for the next day.

Before Barnabas left the shop, Jonathan asked Saul to give all who were present a blessing and a few words from the Scriptures. Saul agreed to do this and quoted a few words from one of the Psalms:

> [11] Let all who take refuge in you rejoice;
>> let them sing joyful praises forever.
> Spread your protection over them,

that all who love your name may be filled with joy.
¹² For you bless the godly, O LORD;
   you surround them with your shield of love.
(Psalm 5.11,12).

This beautiful blessing was from David, who wrote it at the time of the betrayal of his son Absalom. This was a terrifying time for king David, and it was also a terrifying time for Saul of Tarsus, who at that point, had not met any follower of Christ or any apostle, since all were afraid of him.

Barnabas understood how through this Psalm his brother in Christ was conveying his deepest feelings. As he came to know Paul better, the Son of encouragement noticed that Paul often answered a question or gave a word of encouragement by simply quoting from the Scriptures.

As Paul was saying the words of blessing, Barnabas noticed tears swelling up in the eyes of Jonathan the tent maker. Something in these words must have touched the tent maker deeply.

As the bitter cold was falling upon the city, Barnabas walked quickly back home about two miles away. Hiding as best as he could his body and his face from the freezing wind, he was lifting his heart up to God with thanksgiving and praying to God for wisdom for the days ahead.

.

13. PAUL

When Paul first came to Jerusalem, he only met Peter and James, the brother of the Lord. Barnabas went and found Saul and brought him to these two disciples of Jesus. This is also recorded by Luke (Acts 9.26-29). After that, Saul left Jerusalem and was sent by the Church first to Caesarea and then to Tarsus. The strong opposition of the Jewish leaders to the Church ceased for a time, as recorded by Luke, "The church throughout Judea and Galilee and Samaria had peace and was being built up. And walking in the fear of the Lord and in the comfort of the Holy Spirit, it multiplied." (Acts 9.30, 31 ESV). Having left Jerusalem, Paul returned to Tarsus his hometown.

Very early that morning at the first hour of Roman time, Barnabas prayed for Paul, whose life was in danger. He also prayed for Paul to be able to meet with Peter and James, the brother of the Lord. As Barnabas rose up from his time of prayer to God, he felt divine peace in his heart. He knew that the Holy Spirit would guide him and would inspire his words.

Mark had arranged the meeting between the former persecutor of the Church and the two leaders of the Church in Jerusalem. Only Paul and Barnabas were to meet with Peter and James.

The meeting was scheduled at the third hour (9 a.m.) in the humble house of a disciple living in the lower part of the city, thus among the poorest in the population. Peter and James, as all the other apostles, lived very simple lives but received all they needed from the brethren. Since deacons had been chosen to distribute food to the widows, the twelve were giving themselves completely to prayer and the teaching of God's Word. (Acts 6.2).

Mathias had replaced Judas before the Spirit fell on the apostles on the day of Pentecost as promised by Jesus. (Acts 1.15-26).

The Son of encouragement headed towards the upper city to find Paul in the shop of Jonathan, the tentmaker. The day was cold, but the absence of wind made it much milder. Paul also had gotten up very early to pray and write, as was often his custom. Barnabas would learn later that a lot of what Paul was writing at that time was later entrusted to Doctor Luke who would use this information for his book called Acts which follows his Gospel account.

Paul and Barnabas left the shop after enjoying their breakfast with Jonathan and his wife, Abigael. Barnabas was not able to explain to Jonathan where he was taking Paul, since this had to be kept a secret for fear of the religious authorities and for fear of the spies sent to capture the apostles and even Paul.

Barnabas had chosen a time of day close to the sixth hour (noon) to walk towards the lower city. Because the weather was much milder, the streets were full of merchants, people and animals walking either towards the temple or away from it. It was better for the two men to walk among the crowds, rather than at hours when the streets were empty of people but sometimes full of soldiers or tax inspectors, who visited the shops or stopped people on the way, always accompanied by Roman soldiers.

As they walked down to the lower part of the city, Paul and Barnabas saw groups of temple guards wearing clothes different from the Roman soldiers. The Roman soldiers wore vivid colors, but the temple guards did not. However, the temple guards were armed and prepared to deal with thieves or troublemakers, such as the dangerous *sicarii*, especially during the major festivals. The temple guards normally stayed close to the temple, but were on high alert against the followers of Jesus, by order of the religious authorities.

Approaching the poorer section of the city, the two men saw no presence of temple guards but there were Roman soldiers stationed on every street leading to the temple. They turned east into a very narrow street and came to a humble house that had been described by Mark.

Barnabas knocked at the door with a secret number of knocks and the door was opened by an elderly lady, possibly eighty years of age. The small room was only lit by one lantern accompanied by some light coming from a small brazier at the center of the room.

At first, the two men did not see Peter and James, who were seated around a small low table on the left side of the entrance, almost in a corner. The elderly lady made a sign for them to sit by the two men and left the room.

The humble surroundings stood in stark contrast with the importance of this meeting. Barnabas thought *"Will the Lord himself appear to us in person as when he appeared to Saul, to the apostles and even at one time to five hundred brethren? Will the resurrected Jesus come and sit among us?"*

A piece of bread was at the center of the low table. There was also a pitcher with wine and a few cups. The four men were sitting on mats placed on the floor. James raised his hands and thanked God for the safe arrival of the two disciples. Peter took the bread and broke it, sharing it with James, Barnabas and Paul, speaking aloud the beautiful words that had been spoken by the

Lord prior to his crucifixion, "This is my body which is given for you. Do this in remembrance of me."

After they had shared in the bread, James lifted the cup and prayed looking up and saying, "This cup is the new covenant between God and his people and confirmed with my blood which is poured out as a sacrifice for you". (Luke 22.19,20).

As this was happening, Barnabas was watching Paul, wondering if he would be surprised at all by this sharing of the bread and wine and the words of blessing over these elements. But Paul looked like someone who understood exactly what was going on and showed no surprise.

The four disciples of Jesus spent a good part of the day praising the Lord but also talking with Paul about the Lord. As these apostles spoke with Paul, they realized there was nothing they mentioned about the Master that Paul did not already know.

Paul revealed how the Lord had appeared to him on the way to Damascus, his baptism by Ananias and his subsequent preaching in Damascus and his time far away in Arabia for three years.

As the evening was approaching, Peter and James recommended that Paul leave Jerusalem at once, since his life was in danger and his presence was a threat for the thousands of disciples in the city. The plan was for some of the brethren to come very early in the morning and accompany Paul, first to Caesarea on the coast and from there he could sail to Cilicia and travel to his home city of Tarsus.

Barnabas returned home as the sun was rising, remembering these amazing moments and so thankful to God for this brother Paul, whom he found so impressive in his calm demeanor and great knowledge of the Scriptures.

14. BACK TO CYPRUS

Thus, after his brief visit to Jerusalem, Paul returned to Tarsus, his hometown.

The Church in Jerusalem was at peace and praising God from house to house, enjoying an amazing sense of fellowship. Those in greater need were being helped. Many widows received food and shelter under the supervision of the seven deacons appointed by the brethren and apostles. However, at the same time, day-by-day the opposition of the ruling class to the preaching of Christ was growing in intensity.

Many who followed Jesus and lived in Jerusalem were scattered through the regions of Judea and Samaria, except for the apostles. These believers went about preaching the Gospel throughout these regions, fulfilling in this way the words of Christ that the Good News would be preached from Jerusalem in all of Judea and Samaria and to the ends of the earth.

At that time and during the first year of Caligula's rule (37 AD), Barnabas left Jerusalem and moved back to Cyprus with his family. It was winter and not the best time of the year to travel.

The Son of Encouragement decided they would set sail for the Coast of Cilicia and from there to Paphos on the western coast of the island. Even though it took much longer to travel this way, it proved to be a good decision since they learned later that the sea and winds were so rough no boats could sail to the southern coast of the island for a period of almost an entire month.

As Barnabas was slowly approaching the coast of Cyprus, he could distinguish the northern range of the mountains which the people call in Greek *pendaktylos* or "Five finger mountains" and which run parallel to the northern coastline.

From Paphos, it took the family several days to reach Salamis, traveling along the coast, using the amazing roads built by the Romans. They traveled mostly by cart from Paphos which was wholly dedicated to the worship of Aphroditus, the goddess of sexual love and beauty, whom the local population believed was born of sea foam in this region.

After Paphos, the family traveled through the towns of Palaepaphos and Kourion. The luxurious villas of the wealthy, full of marble and mosaics in every room, were scattered all along the coast, on these Roman roads. The family rested in Kourion, an important city-kingdom of Cyprus known for its magnificent theater built over two hundred years before. They then traveled through Amathus and Kithion, finally arriving at Salamis.

On the way they could see displayed the Gentile world of the Greeks and Romans completely given to worshipping false gods and living only for all the pleasures of sensuality without any consideration for God and his Son, the Savior Jesus-Christ.

Despite all the beauty of the creation, the spectacle of the sea, the impressive temples and theaters, as well as so many great works of Roman engineering, one could sense so much darkness and hopelessness, as well as brutality and absence of true love in the lives of these Gentiles. Death was still the destiny of these men and women; without any hope of an eternal home and life with the Father in heaven. In Ecclesiastes, written so long ago, their life was "vapor" and meaningless.

Barnabas did not know it at the time, but a few years later he would be traveling on the same Roman roads, but this time from

Salamis to Paphos, in company of Paul, at the beginning of his first missionary journey.

The family traveled mostly in cold and damp weather. The Son of encouragement often mused over how much had happened to his family. The most significant event had been learning for the first time about the Master, the Lord and Savior Jesus. Sarah and the boys, Elijah and Samuel, had been able to spend time with several of the apostles and all of them had come to faith in the Lord and had been baptized into his name.

Sarah looked forward returning to the farm and getting back together with Esther and her other friends. Elijah and Samuel had grown up to almost adult size and were excited and curious about everything that went on in their travel back to Cyprus. They were discovering the people, landscape, the roads and houses of Cyprus as if they had never seen them.

As they were getting closer to the farm, the boys really started getting excited. When the hill appeared on which the farm was built, they were ready to run up the hill that led to the scenic property overlooking the sea. Eliezer had been informed two weeks before of the arrival of the family, not certain however of the day or time they would be arriving.

Travelers could never be certain of the day or time of arrival except maybe for the special emissaries who traveled on horseback or used the *essedum*, a small car with two wheels and no upper body, closed from the front. The *essedum* is pulled by one or more horses and is a fast way to travel throughout the vast Roman empire. The horses pulling the *essedum* were changed often when travelers needed to go very fast. It is believed that Julius Caesar once traveled in a carriage a distance of eight hundred miles in 8 days. When Nero died, a messenger from Rome carried an urgent message of his death to Galba in Spain in thirty-six hours. Travelers from Rome also used an *itinerarium*, a list of cities and villages with distances between them usually starting from the city of Rome. This helped travelers estimate the time needed to go from one place to another.

Eliezer and his family had been waiting for almost two weeks, barely leaving the house so not to miss the arrival of the family. Food was prepared every day in the hope of their arrival. Barnabas and his family looked forward to meeting the two twin daughters of their friends who now were barely walking at a little over the age of one.

It was late in the afternoon when Barnabas, Sarah and the boys entered the main room of their home lit by two large oil lamps and warmed from the outside cold by a stove at the center of the main room, the dining area.

The dining area had three concrete benches to sit or lie on as the Romans do with several very low tables on which the food was brought. Jewish people would not eat in the homes of the Romans except for business. Barnabas sometimes invited guests of higher rank to the family table, reclining to eat like they would. In Cyprus and many other areas of the Roman Empire, Jews sometimes ate with Gentiles when it was necessary, especially for business discussions.

As Barnabas discussed late into the night with Eliezer, his friend gave him news about the life at the Synagogue. He and his wife Esther were very active within the Jewish community in Salamis and the life of the Synagogue.

Barnabas talked about his experience with the apostles and the claims and teachings of Jesus of Nazareth. Statements made by Jesus were hard for his friend to listen to, such as seeing the Messiah as the manna from heaven, the sacrifice offered for the forgiveness of sins.

The Son of encouragement explained to his friend that the manna and sacrifices that had accompanied Israel through their journey after the deliverance from Egypt were prophecies given to announce the blessings and work of the Messiah, just as the prophets Isaiah or Jeremiah had spoken.

It was clearly difficult for Eliezer to accept Jesus as being the Jewish Messiah.

Spring came and went by quickly with a lot of hard labor working in the fields, taking care of the animals and working on the main house of the farm that needed quite a lot of repair.

However, early that summer Barnabas received an important letter from Jerusalem. The apostles and elders needed someone to go to Antioch and see how the Church was doing. The Church of Antioch had become very large and Barnabas was being asked to travel to Antioch and teach these new converts and encourage them "to remain faithful to the Lord with a steadfast purpose" (Acts 11.19-26).

15. ANTIOCH OF SYRIA

The letter requesting Barnabas travel to Antioch mentioned the growing persecution against believers in Jerusalem after the martyr of Stephen, which had led to a massive exodus from the city into the regions of Phoenicia and even into Antioch of Syria. This was when believers started speaking about Christ to the Greek leaders of the city and a great number believed and were baptized.

At that time Claudius was emperor in Rome. During his thirteen years as Caesar, Claudius greatly expanded the borders of the Roman Empire. It was also under Claudius that Paul and Barnabas, as well as John Mark, were sent on the first missionary journey by the Church in Antioch.

Antioch of Syria had been built east of the Orontes River. This important city was also very close to the Great Sea and was considered one of the most glorious and influential cities in the world. Some even called Antioch the "second Rome".

On the second year of the rule of Caligula (38 AD), by a warm summer day, Barnabas sailed from the eastern coast of Cyprus to Antioch of Syria. He taught in Antioch for three months, after which he traveled to Tarsus of Cilicia to have Paul come and work with the Church at the request of the brethren.

The Romans called Tarsus by the name *Juliopolis*, an important city a short distance from the Great Sea at the mouth of the Cydnus river. Tarsus was always full of merchants and travelers, since it connected the shores of the Great Sea to Cilicia and Anatolia.

After his important meeting with Peter and James, Paul had returned to Tarsus safely. The churches in Judea that are in Christ did not know Paul. Barnabas had prayed very often for

Paul and as he traveled to Antioch of Syria, he determined to go find the apostle in Tarsus and bring him to Antioch.

Barnabas knew that Paul had a special mission given to him by Jesus. He had heard from Paul the words the Lord spoken to him when he appeared to him, "I am Jesus, the one you are persecuting. [16] Now get to your feet! For I have appeared to you to appoint you as my servant and witness. Tell people that you have seen me and tell them what I will show you in the future. [17] And I will rescue you from both your own people and the Gentiles. Yes, I am sending you to the Gentiles [18] to open their eyes, so they may turn from darkness to light and from the power of Satan to God. Then they will receive forgiveness for their sins and be given a place among God's people, who are set apart by faith in me.'" (Acts 26.15-18)

On a beautiful fall day, Barnabas boarded a merchant ship traveling from the Great Sea to Holmoi on the coast of Cilicia. A number of questions haunted him; *how will I be able to convince Paul to return to Jerusalem? How will I even find the apostle to the Gentiles? How will Paul be able to reach the Gentiles throughout the Roman Empire?*

At that point, Barnabas had no idea that God would call him, along with the apostle Paul to accomplish this mission. He had been able to lead Saul to Peter and James the brother of Jesus. However, the fear of Saul of Tarsus had taken years to subside among the brethren in Jerusalem and throughout Judea.

As he traveled to Tarsus, Barnabas carried with him the letter given to him by the church in Antioch. As a Roman citizen and known in the business world, Barnabas knew he could enter the province of Cilicia and travel on the Roman roads or on

Roman ships without any trouble from the authorities or the soldiers stationed in this province. Cilicia was one of the most important regions of Anatolia and in the past was under the rule of peoples known as Hittites and even of Armenians.

A great highway from the west came from the Anatolian plateau to the city of Tarsus. This famous road ran through the narrow pass between walls of rock called the Cilician Gates, a pass through the Taurus Mountains connecting the low plains of Cilicia to the Anatolian plateau. The Cilician Gates saw a constant flow of merchants and Roman soldiers.

Cilicia used to export the goats-hair cloth known as *Cilicium* which were used to make tents. Saul, from Tarsus, the capital city of Cilicia, had been by trade a tent maker all the while having been trained as a teacher of the Law under Gamaliel in Jerusalem. That is why he was present at the stoning of Stephen in Jerusalem, even keeping his clothes as the deacon was being stoned to death.

Barnabas had been sailing for a little over a week when he reached the coast of Cilicia. It would take him two more days to reach Tarsus. The road to Tarsus had been built by the Romans and travelers who could afford the cost were able to use carts instead of walking, thus reducing the time to travel to about two days instead of one week.

Tarsus offered a number of advantages to its citizens. The city had been exempted from taxation under Augustus because Athenodorus, the teacher and friend of the emperor was from Tarsus. A number of the Greek teachers of stoicism had lived in Tarsus such as Athenodorus, Zeno and Antipater. The city was an important center of learning for the Greeks and Romans as well as Jews.

After he encountered the Lord on the road to Damascus, the apostle Paul had preached and taught in the Syrian city and in Arabia for three years before briefly visiting Jerusalem and meeting with Peter and James along with Barnabas. He then returned to his hometown and worked in a tent making shop.

As Barnabas was coming closer to Tarsus, he felt a great burden on his shoulders and prayed unceasingly. He was looking forward to meeting with Paul again after several years had passed. The Son of encouragement was now about 45 years of age and Paul was about ten years younger than him.

Barnabas entered the gates of Tarsus at sunset. He checked with the soldiers about the reason for his visit. He would be staying with a man by the name of Joseph and his family, himself a Levite and a member of one of the main synagogues.

Barnabas was bringing two jars of his best olive oil as a gift for the family. Joseph was a merchant who traded with the fishing companies on the coast who sold their fish to several merchants in the city. He traveled a lot back and forth to the sea for his business. His wife's name was Avital and they had two boys and a girl, the three of them under the age of ten.

Barnabas arrived two days before the Sabbath and decided to stay with Joseph and his family through the Sabbath and attend the Synagogue. Joseph, being a Levite, was chosen as the second reader of the Torah that day. The second reading was from Genesis where we read that the Lord appeared to Abraham by the oaks of Mamre. (Genesis 18.1-10). This was when the promise to Abraham was renewed and one of the men visiting Abraham said to him, "Where is your wife Sarah?" And he said, "There, in the tent." Then one said, "I will surely return to you in due season, and your wife Sarah shall have a son.".

Later that day, Barnabas asked Joseph what he thought about the promises made to Abraham and Sarah and he discussed this at length with his friend. In the conversation, Barnabas mentioned his cousin Mark and how he now followed the teaching of Jesus of Nazareth. Joseph had always shown an interest in the discussions between different schools of interpretation. He was very surprised that a Rabbi like Jesus would choose as disciples a few fishermen and even a tax collector. Joseph was well acquainted with fishermen and this aspect of the story of Jesus was fascinating to him.

As they talked late into the night, Barnabas realized that for Joseph, the story of Jesus as a teacher was unique, and Jesus himself was very unlike other teachers. During these discussions with his friend, Barnabas asked about tent makers in Tarsus and Joseph knew some of them. He planned, the next day, to go and visit with some of the tent makers and find out about Saul.

Tarsus was known for its tent makers and all the trades related to this business. Barnabas had traveled to Tarsus several times in the past and had no difficulty in finding Paul at his work in one of the shops of the city, just as he had found him in Jerusalem fifteen years before.

Paul had not changed much since their short encounter in Jerusalem. The only thing different was that he was clearly losing a lot of hair. None of his passion and ability to teach seemed in any way diminished. This man was a ball of energy in a feeble frame, a strong man with a weak appearance. He did not have a very loud or powerful voice, but his speech would usually bring about silence and great attention.

Paul would quote Scripture so accurately and easily that Barnabas did not cease to be impressed by the man. He did not use any crude joking as sometimes happened in his trade but remained very careful with his words. His demeanor was strangely impressive although he was small in stature and very slim. He spoke Hebrew, Aramaic, Greek and Latin fluently. He knew the teachings of the Pharisees and Sadducees. He knew of the teachings of Aristotle and Plato and other Greek authors.

This man had a wealth of knowledge which seemed limitless. However, anybody meeting him for the first time might think he was just a tent maker, like many others with very little education, since his demeanor was always very humble and he never, like so many other teachers, displayed any kind of arrogance, despite his impressive knowledge.

Seeing Paul and being in his company was always a heart-warming experience for Barnabas. No words can explain how powerfully the Holy Spirit guided every aspect of his person and of his life. He was truly following the Lord Jesus in a way Barnabas had not seen in anybody else except the apostles of Jesus. The fruit of the Spirit was obvious, both in his actions and words.

It took Paul and Barnabas ten days to return to Antioch. The apostle Paul was warmly received by the brethren, who for the most part had been converted from the Greek speaking Gentiles. The apostle Paul would be a great teacher for them because of his knowledge both of Judaism and of the Gentile world.

After a year in Antioch, Barnabas decided to sell his farm and all lands to work with the Church as a teacher and evangelist. Sarah and the boys moved to Antioch. The Son of encouragement sold Eliezer the farm and gave him most of the land.

After Sarah and the boys moved to Antioch, the Church grew even more and numbered several prophets and teachers whose names were Simeon also called Niger, Lucius of Cyrene, Manaen, a lifelong friend of Herod the Tetrach.

Saul and Barnabas were also teachers for the congregation (Acts 13.1,2).

Claudius was emperor and a great famine took over Judea during the 5th and 6th years of his rule. The church in Antioch collected funds. Saul and Barnabas brought financial relief to the elders in Jerusalem for the brethren in Judea. With this help, food could be purchased in areas as far as Alexandria to help feed the brethren and churches. (Acts 11.27-30)

This was also when king Herod II, also known as Agrippa I and the grandson of Herod the Great, had James the brother of John killed in Jerusalem, as well as other brethren. This was done with the approval of Ananus, the High Priest at the time.

Agrippa I died in a striking manner. Having ruled for three years, he came to Caesarea for a celebration in honor of Caesar and on that occasion the people of Tyre and Sidon came to appease the king whom they had displeased. On the day of their meeting, Agrippa was wearing a garment made of silver. He came early in the morning in the theater and the sun completely illuminated the silver of his garment. The crowds cried out to him that he was a god and begged for his mercy. Immediately a severe pain came into his belly, and he was carried to the palace and was in pain for five days. He died at the age of 44 in the 7th year of his reign.

16. THE MISSION

On an early summer day, the prophets and teachers of the Church in Antioch were praying and fasting along with many others. It was revealed to all of them through the Holy Spirit that Saul and Barnabas should be set apart and sent off into the Gentile world beyond Syria. At that time Mark had come to Antioch to help the leaders of the Church and joined this mission. This was during the 7th year of the rule of Claudius.

The Spirit, through God's Word, had already taught the Church to go and preach the Gospel to all the nations. This was the mission that Jesus had given to his apostles during his forty days of teaching after he rose from the dead. (Acts 1). There was really nothing new about this. However, the Spirit also works in giving discernment and wisdom in very practical matters such as choosing leaders, teachers or elders.

Thus, it appeared to the congregation in Antioch and its leaders under the guidance of the Spirit, that Paul and Barnabas should go out from the Church into these areas where the Gospel had not yet been proclaimed. Mark would also accompany them as a helper.

The congregation provided these men with enough funds to be able to travel for at least a year. They also carried with them a Roman *itinerarium*, a document in Latin which provided travelers with distance calculations of the main towns relative to Rome. This would allow these preachers to plan according to the distance they would travel. They also believed that the Lord himself would show them which towns would be more open to the Gospel and which ones would not be that acccepting. This was not something they could or needed to be concerned with. As taught by Jesus, they were going as sowers of the Word of the Master, realizing each human heart would respond differently; knowing that all they could do was to sow and water the Word, but only God could give the increase and bring people to faith, obedience and spiritual growth.

Three days later Paul, Mark and Barnabas boarded a ship from Seleucia. The distance between Seleucia and Cyprus would require several days of sailing, hoping that the Great Sea would not be dangerous.

The three of them watched from the rear of the boat as the ship slowly cruised from the coast. Family members as well as many of the brethren had come to Seleucia to say farewell and pray with these men at their departure.

Initially, they were not going to travel in territory completely foreign to them. Barnabas was of course very familiar with Cyprus. Paul had lived many years in Cilicia and had also traveled some through the area. For Mark, however, this territory was completely new. The three of them had Roman citizenship, which would be a great advantage, as they would certainly encounter Roman soldiers traveling on the roads or guarding the gates of some of the cities.

Travelers would usually travel in groups of at least seven and armed, especially if they were carrying merchandise or money. Roman soldiers were also assigned to specific areas where thieves could rob travelers, even kill them. They had prayed about this but still chose to be only three traveling together in often dangerous territory.

The three Christians landed in Salamis one afternoon on the day of preparation (Friday) which is the day prior to the Sabbath. The weather was very hot. As soon as they landed, they sat under a large cedar tree, some distance from the beach, in order to rest, pray and eat dried figs and bread they had brought.

Many short and wild olive trees had grown here and there around them. These wild olive trees were more like shrubs and could be found all over the island. These olive trees were much smaller than the cultivated olive trees which can attain a height of fifteen meters. The white flowers of the cultivated olive trees started to open in the Spring and provided a sweet smell which could linger for many weeks, while the olives themselves ripened around the ninth month of the Roman calendar (November).

After resting for a couple of hours, they started walking to Salamis, hoping to find some lodging. Ruben and his wife Rebecca, friends of Barnabas, welcomed them. Ruben was a true man of peace, a godly Jew who cultivated grapes. A dozen fig trees had grown around his modest dwelling. Ruben and Barnabas had not seen each other now for many years and their children were all grown up. Their home was modest since they were not among the wealthier families of this area, but they had this great gift of hospitality and provided food and lodging for the three Christian preachers.

At the dinner table that evening, Ruben and Rebecca heard with amazement the teachings of Paul and the story of his encounter with Jesus. They recognized in him a great teacher of the Scriptures and Ruben invited Paul to come and speak at the synagogue of Salamis the next day, which was the Sabbath.

When they arrived at the , everyone welcomed the three men with joy. The reading of the day was from the fifth book of the law called *devarim* (Deuteronomy) and the text was the promise made to Moses that God would raise up a prophet greater than him to teach and lead the people. (Deuteronomy 18). The leaders of the synagogue did not show opposition to Paul's preaching but did not seem willing to hear more about it.

Leaving the next day, Paul, Barnabas and Mark walked for about three hours and reached the famous road built along part of the southern coast of Cyprus and which runs through the towns of Kition, Amathus and Kourion. After five days, they finally entered the town of Paphos on the western side of Cyprus from where they would sail for the coast of Pamphylia.

As they walked on the Roman road leading to Paphos, they did not know at the time that believers in the Lord were already living in the towns of Kition and Kourion. These Christians had come back to Cyprus, their homeland, all the way from Jerusalem after the stoning of Stephen and the persecution against the Church, including the one instigated by Paul before his conversion.

It was only after all his travels with Paul that Barnabas learned about the presence of these Christians on Cyprus. (Acts 11.19). This was an example for these three men of how God works, even through opposition and enemies of the faith, to produce good in this world. They were reminded of the words of Joseph to his brothers who wanted to kill him and sell him as a slave to Egypt, "[19] Don't be afraid of me. Am I God, that I can punish you? [20] You intended to harm me, but God intended it all for good. He brought me to this position so I could save the lives of many people. [21] No, don't be afraid. I will continue to take care of you and your children." So, he reassured them by speaking kindly to them." (Genesis 50.20).

Entering the gates of Paphos, a Roman soldier summoned the three Christians to meet with the proconsul of this entire region, Sergius Paulus. They knew by the manner in which the proconsul was reaching out to them that he did not have bad intentions towards them. Only men of the highest social rank could rule entire provinces and receive appointments on behalf of Rome. Cyprus was a senatorial province, and it was the senate that appointed a proconsul to rule the island each year. Paphos was an important seat of power and had been chosen by Rome as its capital city on Cyprus. The proconsul was regularly informed of any news concerning the Roman world.

The proconsul's villa, situated on a small elevation, was more like a palace with marble everywhere and Greek and Roman statues in each room as well as the main courtyard. The large villa was attached to several farms and like many others, was self-sufficient, providing food for the proconsul and his family as well as for the slaves and some freedmen working for him. All of this was happening during the seventh year of the rule of Claudius who reigned in Rome for almost fourteen years and was replaced by Nero. It was also two years after the great famine that devastated Judea during the fifth and sixth year of Claudius' rule. This famine occurred a year after Barnabas went to Tarsus to bring Paul to Antioch.

Sergius Paulus received Paul, Barnabas and Mark in one of the heated rooms of the villa, since the weather was cool that day. He was sitting with four members of his staff on chairs in a circular fashion. Beside him was Elymas, a magician also known as Bar-Jesus, who claimed to be a prophet from God.

The apostle Paul spoke to Sergius Paulus from the Scriptures and preached to him Jesus as the Messiah, fulfilling the law and the prophets. Like many other Roman dignitaries or soldiers, the proconsul was not ignorant of the Jewish Scriptures. Gentiles were often seen attending the synagogues and were sometimes known as "God fearers", even without becoming proselytes of the Jewish faith.

As the apostle Paul was teaching from the Scriptures and explaining how Jesus was the Messiah, Elymas interrupted him several times and tried to convince the proconsul that Paul was lying. At last, the apostle looked at Elymas and spoke stern words to the magician, even calling him "son of the devil" and "enemy of all righteousness", adding: "Will you not stop making crooked the straight paths of the Lord? (Acts 13.10 ESV).

As Barnabas heard this statement from Paul, he was reminded of the Scripture from Proverbs,

> "[12] Wisdom will save you from evil people,
>   from those whose words are twisted.
> [13] These men turn from the right way
>   to walk down dark paths.
> [14] They take pleasure in doing wrong,
>   and they enjoy the twisted ways of evil.
> [15] Their actions are crooked,
>   and their ways are wrong."
> (Proverbs 2.12-15)

As soon as Paul had pronounced these words, the magician became blind. Having lost his sight, he went about in the room not knowing where to go and finally was guided out by one of the servants of the proconsul.

The three preachers stayed for three weeks in the area and were informed that Elymas had recovered his eyesight.

Sergius Paulus became a believer in Jesus, fulfilling the words Jesus had spoken to the apostle Paul on the way to Damascus who himself had become blind at his encounter with the Lord: "Yes, I am sending you to the Gentiles [18] to open their eyes, so they may turn from darkness to light and from the power of Satan to God. Then they will receive forgiveness for their sins and be given a place among God's people, who are set apart by faith in me.' (Acts 26.17,18).

At the end of those three weeks, they departed Cyprus and sailed to Perga on the coast of Pamphylia. From there they would head to Antioch of Pisidia where they planned to attend the synagogue. Pamphylia extends from the Great Sea to the Taurus mountains. The Greek writers believed that the people from Pamphylia came to this region with the famous Greek soothsayer Calchas after the Trojan war.

They needed to sail 200 miles to reach Perga and were able to find a commercial boat carrying mostly wine and which had room only for eight passengers. When they reached the coast, the three of them walked to the town of Perga seven miles inland up the Kestros river. As soon as they reached land, Mark informed Paul and Barnabas that he wanted to return to Jerusalem. So, Mark left the two other men. Later, Paul did not want Mark on his second missionary journey, stating because he had deserted them in Pamphylia and did not continue with them in their travels. When, however, when he was a prisoner in Rome, Paul wrote to Timothy asking him to come to Rome and to bring Mark along with him as a "useful servant" (2 Timothy 4.11).

17. ANTIOCH IN PISIDIA

Traveling north from the region of Pamphylia towards the region of Pisidia, Paul and Barnabas were heading to a higher elevation. This would take several weeks and bring them closer to the winter months. As they walked, the warmer climate subsided day by day and the nights especially became much colder.

The two preachers were leaving the world of Roman domination and reaching into populations less influenced by the Romans, as far as their gods and religion, as well as the power struggles of the time. According to the Greek writers, Pisidia had not, even in the past, come under the control of the powerful Hittites. Even the Persians, when they conquered Anatolia, attempted to rule Pisidia by dividing it in satrapies but had very little control of the area according to the ancient Greek writers.

The rainfall in Pisidia was more significant and thus benefited the soil, making it fertile for growing fruit and for abundant grazing of sheep and goats. A number of lakes were scattered throughout the area. The towns of Pisidia were, for the most part, built on the slopes in order to benefit from the fertility brought about by the rain. According to ancient Greek writers, Pisidia had approximately population as Pamphylia. It was a mountainous region and known for being more difficult for outside powers to rule. The people of Pisidia were known for their greater independence in their way of life and Rome's presence was not felt by the local population as much as other areas.

In its efforts to try and control the region, Rome ordered the construction of the famous paved road, the *Via Sebaste*. It was at Antioch of Pisidia that the *Via Sebaste* separated into two directions for the southwest and southeast. The Romans even built secondary connecting roads between these two roads. The location of the Roman roads played a big part in traveling plans during these missionary journeys. The churches, which were established in Antioch, Lystra, Derbe and Iconium, could at that time be spoken of as part of Galatia and would include the brethren addressed in Paul's letter to the Galatians.

There was a large synagogue in Antioch that served the needs of not only the Jews but also the proselytes and the Gentile God-fearers in the population. The God-fearers attended the synagogue without having become proselytes of Judaism. The Antioch Synagogue was the one Paul wanted to reach as he knew we would be invited to speak there on the Sabbath.

After the usual readings of the law and the prophets, Paul and Barnabas were invited by the rulers of the Synagogue with these words, "Brothers, if you have any word of encouragement for the people, come and give it." (Acts 13.15). Without any hesitation Paul rose from his seat, walked to the podium, and spoke to the large crowd gathered to hear him. He recalled the biblical account of how God, from the time he chose the ancestors of the people of Israel, made them multiply and grow in Egypt and through his great power delivered them. Paul also described how the people were in the desert forty years and finally entered the promised land and later what happened at the time of the Judges. He continued with the history of Israel until God chose David to rule over them and made a covenant with him.

The apostle then described the birth of Jesus and the preaching of repentance by John the Baptist who proclaimed to the people, 'Do you think I am the Messiah? No, I am not! But he is coming soon—and I'm not even worthy to be his slave and untie the sandals on his feet.'

The apostle continued his speech, saying: "Men of Israel and you God-fearing Gentiles, listen to me. [17] "The God of this nation of Israel chose our ancestors and made them multiply and grow strong during their stay in Egypt. Then with a powerful arm he led them out of their slavery.

"After that, God gave them judges to rule until the time of Samuel the prophet. [21] Then the people begged for a king, and God gave them Saul son of Kish, a man of the tribe of Benjamin, who reigned for forty years. [22] But God removed Saul and replaced him with David, a man about whom God said, 'I have found David son of Jesse, a man after my own heart. He will do everything I want him to do.'

[23] "And it is one of King David's descendants, Jesus, who is God's promised Savior of Israel! [24] Before he came, John the Baptist preached that all the people of Israel needed to repent of their sins and turn to God."

The apostle continued his speech with the following words: [26] "Brothers—you sons of Abraham, and you God-fearing Gentiles—this message of salvation has been sent to us! [27] The people in Jerusalem and their leaders did not recognize Jesus as the one the prophets had spoken about. Instead, they condemned him, and in doing this they fulfilled the prophets' words that are read every Sabbath. [28] They found no legal reason to execute him, but they asked Pilate to have him killed anyway.

The apostle continued to speak saying, "[34]God had promised to raise him from the dead, not leaving him to rot in the grave. He said, 'I will give you the sacred blessings I promised to David.' [35] Another psalm explains it more fully: 'You will not allow your Holy One to rot in the grave.' [36] This is not a reference to David, for after David had done the will of God in his own generation, he died and was buried with his ancestors, and his body decayed. [37] No, it was a reference to someone else—someone whom God raised and whose body did not decay. [38] "Brothers, listen! We are here to proclaim that through this man Jesus there is forgiveness for your sins. [39] Everyone who believes in him is made right in God's sight—something the law of Moses could never do." (Acts 13.16-39)

After this long speech, Paul went back to his seat. The service was adjourned following the singing of several Psalms. Many of the Jews and Gentiles came to the two Christian preachers wanting to speak to them more. They asked Paul and Barnabas to return the next Sabbath to speak again.

Following this Sabbath assembly at the synagogue, Paul and Barnabas were warmly welcomed into the home of a generous family and were invited from house to house to teach about the Gospel of Jesus Christ.

On the second Sabbath in Antioch, great numbers both of Jews and Gentiles came to hear Paul. As Paul had just started speaking from the podium, some of the religious leaders started shouted to contradict him and interrupt him especially as he mentioned the salvation of the Gentiles. The apostle reminded them how the Messiah would come as a light to the Gentiles according to the prophet Isaiah, "I have made you a light to the Gentiles, that you may bring salvation to the ends of the earth." (Isaiah 49.6; Acts 13.47).

The Gentiles, however, wanted to hear more of Paul's words. Many rejoiced about the Good News of God's salvation and many of them believed in Christ. Paul and Barnabas stayed as long as they could in this area, teaching a great number. A great number of Gentiles came to faith in Jesus and salvation.

This happened during the 8th year of the rule of Claudius. It was impossible to travel in the winter, Antioch being at an altitude of 3500 feet. Iconium about 90 miles away was at an altitude of 3300 feet. Thus, Paul and Barnabas spent a good part of the winter in Antioch and the area, encouraging the believers to stay faithful to the Word and God's grace, despite strong opposition which finally led the leaders of the city to force them to leave.

When Paul was a prisoner in Rome at the end of his earthly life, he wrote to the evangelist Timothy the following words: "[10] But you, Timothy, certainly know what I teach, and how I live, and what my purpose in life is. You know my faith, my patience, my love, and my endurance. [11] You know how much persecution and suffering I have endured. You know all about how I was persecuted in Antioch, Iconium, and Lystra—but the Lord rescued me from all of it. [12] Yes, and everyone who wants to live a godly life in Christ Jesus will suffer persecution. [13] But evil people and impostors will flourish. They will deceive others and will themselves be deceived." (2 Timothy 3.10-13)

Barnabas witnessed this faith of the apostle of Jesus, his patience, love and endurance required of God's servants, men or women, young or old, not only of apostles. As they traveled along these perilous roads and preached the Gospel, they met rejection and violence by some but also gratitude and good will from others. In all of this, it was crucial for them to maintain their faith and to act and speak with patience and love towards all. In fact, is was in Lystra that Timothy became a believer and was taught the plan of God for the salvation of mankind. Later on, this young man became an evangelist, who at times accompanied the apostle Paul along with Silas.

18. ICONIUM

The two men left Antioch very early one morning near the beginning of March. The believers, both Jews and Gentiles, provided them with food and some funds to travel and tearfully saw
them walk away.

The lives of these new believers had been completely transformed by what they had heard and learned. Paul and Barnabas
had encountered strong opposition in Antioch and knew this
would also be the case for these new believers. They encouraged
them to continue in the faith, to be persistent in following the
teachings of the Master and to remember his death and resurrection by sharing in the Lord's supper.

The two men pursued their missionary voyage towards the
south-east into the Phrygian valley. This region was also considered part of Galatia. As they travelled, they noticed many
of the monumental tombs the Phrygian people had carved in
the soft volcanic rock of this land. According to Greek legend,
king Midas, who turned everything he touched into gold, was a
Phrygian king.

The cold weather had mostly subsided. To reach Iconium,
they needed to travel ninety miles. They were able to travel on
the amazing roads built by the Romans and especially the *Via
Sebaste*, the main road connecting the Roman colonies of this region. The road was well built and paved and could accommodate
wheeled carts traveling to Iconium and Lystra.

Paul and Barnabas were able to travel on a cart all the way
from Antioch of Pisidia to Iconium having been provided with
enough funding for this expense.

They finally entered the town of Iconium late in the afternoon, very tired and hungry. The city had been built at the foot of Mount Taurus and was the capital city of Lycaonia. It was an important city since it was situated on the main Roman road that goes from Ephesus to Tarsus and all the way to the Euphrates.

Iconium and the surrounding area were known for growing apricots, cotton, flax and grapes used in the production of wine. This was a fertile plain surrounded by mountains. The presence of the Romans was quite visible, but there were no real conflicts with the Roman rulers at that time. Iconium had been a part of the Roman province of Asia for over a hundred and forty years, thus there was a strong military presence of Rome in this city. Under the Roman rule, the city had prospered, which was partly due to the great road constructions allowing easy travel and the development of commerce throughout and beyond Asia.

Samuel, a prominent member of the synagogue, and his wife Rebecca, greeted the two men warmly, having heard about them from family members living in Antioch. The couple owned several acres of apricot trees. These apricots were sold throughout the city and in the area. They also owned quite a lot of livestock. Samuel was a man with a keen interest in the Scriptures, especially as they pertain to the promised Messiah. Having heard about Paul, who had studied under Gamaliel, and about Barnabas, a Levite from Cyprus, both Samuel and Rebecca were eager to visit with the two men. The disposition and hospitality of this couple greatly warmed the hearts of the apostle and his companion.

As they sat on the ground at the low dinner table, Samuel gave the blessing and quoting from the words of Psalm 96:

"⁴ Great is the LORD! He is most worthy of praise!
    He is to be feared above all gods.
⁵ The gods of other nations are mere idols,
    but the LORD made the heavens!
⁶ Honor and majesty surround him;
    strength and beauty fill his sanctuary.
⁷ O nations of the world recognize the LORD;
    recognize that the LORD is glorious and strong."
(Psalm 96.1-7)

The two preachers conversed with Samuel and Rebecca, pointing out that one of the greatest obstacles to their teaching was the message of the cross itself, which remained a symbol of infamy and cruelty on the part of the Roman conquerors.

Another obstacle was the inclusion of Gentiles into God's covenant. Paul quoted the Scriptures and recalled how often God promised blessings to the Gentiles through His people Israel and through the Messiah. In fact, the Psalm Samuel quoted for the blessing was all about this theme of God calling the Gentiles into fellowship with him.

In their discussion, it also became clear that a great obstacle for their Jewish brethren would be the setting aside of circumcision and the law of Moses as a requirement for Gentiles to receive God's blessings and favor.

The synagogue in Iconium was comprised of a large Jewish community and also of Gentiles who believed in the one God of Israel and wanted to receive instruction in the Scriptures. They were called "God fearers". Only a handful of these Gentiles of Iconium had become Jewish proselytes and had been circumcised to be able to enter the covenant with the God of Israel.

Circumcision was a great obstacle for Gentiles who had slaves or freedmen working under them or who were in an official position with the local authorities. When it was known that these Gentiles had been circumcised and joined into the covenant of Israel, they often lost all respect from those under them.

There was the fear that Gentile slaves who became Christians and formerly who worshipped the pagan gods of their masters would cease to respect their masters. There was a famous case like that with the conversion to Judaism of Helena, the queen of Adiabene and her son Izates. The son of Helena met a Jewish merchant, whose name was Ananias, who taught him to worship the only God, the creator of the world. When his mother, Helena learned about this, she dissuaded her son from embracing the Jewish faith and being circumcised, arguing that if he did, his subjects would hate him and reject his authority. Izates, however, talked with other teachers of Judaism who were successful in convincing him to come into the covenant and to receive circumcision, which he did. When Izates received circumcision, none of his subjects, slaves or freedmen despised him. When Helena saw this, she herself entered the covenant and came to live under the law of Moses.

They talked for several hours late into the night about this great obstacle to the preaching of the Gospel, both for the Jewish brethren and for the Gentiles.

When the Gentiles who had been attending the synagogue heard that through faith in the Jewish Messiah they could be adopted into the family of God and receive His blessings, they rejoiced greatly and came to faith. That is why in Antioch, a great number of Gentiles had come to believe and receive salvation, by faith in Jesus' name.

Paul and Barnabas also talked about how Peter had been sent by God to the family of Cornelius, the centurion of Caesarea, and how God showed him the foods not allowed to eat under the law and told him, "Rise, Peter, kill and eat." Peter objected to this, but the Lord came to him and repeated three times the same thing, concluding with this statement, "What God has made clean, do not call common." In his Gospel account, Mark later testified about the Lord's teachings in the matter of food, saying, "Can't you see that the food you put into your body cannot defile you? [19] Food doesn't go into your heart, but only passes through the stomach and then goes into the sewer." (By saying this, he declared that every kind of food is acceptable in God's eyes.) [20] And then he added, "It is what comes from inside that defiles you. [21] For from within, out of a person's heart, come evil thoughts, sexual immorality, theft, murder, [22] adultery, greed, wickedness, deceit, lustful desires, envy, slander, pride, and foolishness. [23] All these vile things come from within; they are what defile you." (Mark 7.18-23).

Paul and Barnabas reached Iconium two days before the Sabbath. They were looking forward to their first Sabbath. This was in March of the 8th year of Claudius' rule over Rome (48 AD).

It was a beautiful spring day, very appropriate for declaring the resurrected Lord and the salvation he had brought to the world. The readings at the Synagogue were from Exodus, the passage about the altar of incense (Exodus 30.1-10) and from Ezekiel's prophecy about the promise of God's Spirit given to all in order to create in them a new heart and a new spirit. (Ezekiel 36.22-32).

The apostle Paul and Barnabas were invited to speak about these texts of the Law and Prophets.

The two preachers explained how these readings in Exodus and in the prophecy Ezekiel were prophetical of the salvation and blessings offered by God through his anointed one, the Messiah of Israel.

As soon as the service was over, there was quite a lot of turmoil in the large assembly of Jewish brethren and the few Gentiles present. Some of the Jewish leaders rejected the preaching of a crucified Messiah, which they considered shameful to teach both to Jews and Gentiles.

Moreover, it did not seem possible for them that God would embrace Gentiles and offer them forgiveness only on the basis of faith in the Lord Jesus without submitting entirely to the Law, including circumcision.

At the same time, a great number in this assembly were enthralled by the message and believed in Jesus as the Messiah as well as Savior of Israel and the nations.

The two preachers stayed in Iconium teaching from house to house every day. Samuel and his wife Rebecca became believers in Christ.

Every day, in Iconium, more Gentiles came to faith in Jesus with gladness. After three Sabbaths, Paul and Barnabas were no longer able attend the Synagogue. The city was divided because of their teaching. The message of the grace God offered through Jesus had become a message that divided the population and even families.

Through March and April, weeks went by with more Jews and Gentiles coming to faith in Christ. The Lord allowed Paul to heal some who were blind, to pray for those who were sick, and many were healed. The apostle and Barnabas ministered in Iconium until the end of July.

They had left Antioch of Syria over a year before. Barnabas greatl missed his wife Sarah. Their two sons were now married and had children. Mark had returned to Antioch and later to Jerusalem.

The first week of the month of August, Paul and Barnabas were informed one evening that a group of Jews and Gentiles were planning to kill them by stoning as soon as an opportunity would arise.

At that very hour enabled by a full moon, they left the house of Samuel and Rebecca with two of their servants who would be guiding them through the nearby mountains. They were heading to Lystra, which could also be reached through the main Roman road. However, the four men avoided the highway at first. Providentially, the weather was warm, and the full moon allowed their guides to find their way through the narrow mountain paths.

Paul, Barnabas and the two servants reached the Roman road leading to Lystra, which continues towards Tarsus. They felt great relief to come down to the plains and join the paved highway. They would need to walk south all the way to Lystra, since they had not been able to find a cart to take them to this city.

Reaching the Roman highway early in the morning, they found a quiet spot close to the highway where they rested for two or three hours and ate dried figs and bread their guides had carried with them. Once they had rested, the two guides left them and walked back to Iconium using the highway.

It took Paul and Barnabas two more days walking on the highway to finally reach Lystra. In those two days of travel, they encountered only a group of about forty Roman soldiers who were traveling by cart, as well as merchants on a larger cart bringing goods to Lystra. The merchants would have offered help, had they not been carrying a full cart of wine, olives and figs. However, the two men were able to purchase some food from these traveling merchants, as well as enough water for a few days

19. LYSTRA

Lystra was an important city in the region of Lycaonia, south of Iconium, located on the famous Roman road the *Via Sebaste* that runs from Ephesus to Antioch in Pisidia. The road continues from Lystra and Derbe through the Cilician Gates and then to Tarsus and finally to Antioch in Syria. The city had been incorporated by Rome into the Province of Galatia. It was a Roman colony with Roman administration.

Rome started building these roads centuries before the Empire existed, even under the Republic. Roads like the *Via Sebaste* followed the natural communication routes that had existed throughout history. They were made of quarried stones and had bridges built to cross riverbeds and depressions. The Romans also used fixed stones to mark distances. A good part of the road construction under Rome was the work of the military. Their purpose was to facilitate the movement of the Roman legions. They also carried pagan pilgrims to important places of worship, such as the temple of Artemis in Ephesus or the temple of Asclepius in Pergamum (Acts 19.24-26). The Jewish pilgrims also used *Via Sebaste* and other roads to reach Jerusalem.

The region of Lycaonia was Hellenized under the rule of the Seleucids after the death of Alexander the Great. The Lycaonian language was Greek intermingled with Syriac, which allowed Paul and Barnabas to understand it. The Lycaonians had adopted Greek mythology as the basis of their religion. Some of these people were well versed in Roman authors such as Ovid's Metamorphosis, which deals with Mercury and Jupiter (Hermes and Zeus for the Greeks). In these writings, Mercury and Jupiter are described as visiting their area.

Lystra had been built over a steep hill bordered by a stream which flowed partly into a cistern from where the inhabitants could draw water. At the outskirts of Lystra, one could see a lightly wooded area. From the top of the city, one could see bare and rolling hills. Livestock in this area were mainly sheep and donkeys and were used in many ways. The city was full of narrow streets and full of temples, with baths and public buildings. The temple of Jupiter (the Greek God Zeus) stood at the entrance of the gates of the city.

Lystra would be an important city in Paul's mission travels. A little over two years after this first visit to Lystra, the apostle and his companion, Silas returned to these regions during this return visit through Lystra and Iconium. through Lystra and Iconium. Timothy was called by Paul to travel with him. Timothy's mother was Jewish and had come to the faith and his father was Greek. (Acts 16.1-3; 2 Timothy 3.11).

Paul and Barnabas already knew from their brethren in Iconium that Lystra did not have a synagogue. The Jewish community in Lystra was small and did not have the required number of Jews to form a synagogue, which is at least ten male members. This would be the first place reached during their missionary voyage where the two Christians would be speaking to the Gentiles without approaching them through a synagogue.

As Paul and Barnabas had almost reached the gates of Lystra, they found along the road a *mansiones* — sort of inn — where they could eat and rent a room for a night or more. This *mansiones* was large and had several rooms and even a large dining area comprised of tables and chairs and a L shaped marble counter about eight feet long. Two large potteries stood on the counter containing dried fruit. Behind the counter stood two large amphorae containing wine. A man and a woman were cooking food on a simple brazier. The owners wanted to be paid in Roman coins and the brethren in Antioch and Iconium had provided Paul and Barnabas with coins used mainly in the province of Lycaonia. These coins had the letters IMPE AUGUSTI at their head and were stamped with the portrait of Augustus and the letters COL IVL/ FEL CEM LYSTRA at the back. The name Lystra was represented by a priest standing and plowing with yoke and oxen while holding an ornate staff in the left hand.

Early the next day, after they had been able to rest from their travels, Paul and his companion headed towards the gates of the city of Lystra. Only a short distance from their *mansiones,* the worshippers of Zeus had erected a large temple in honor of the Greek god (Jupiter for the Romans). Just before entering the pagan temple grounds, beggars could be found, usually crippled individuals.

Without entering the grounds, the two men approached the entrance to the massive temple dedicated to one of the chief deities of these people. They could smell the burning of incense and animals within the main courtyard. They walked by an older man who was crippled and could not walk. Family members or friends would bring crippled individuals close to the entrance of the temple on certain days when they expected more pilgrims to visit the temple of Zeus.

This often happened because the writings of Ovid mention the legend of Zeus and Hermes visiting their area. There was always the hope that at some point these two gods would show up again and heal the sick.

The apostle Paul stood on one of the large stones by the entrance of the courtyard and spoke loudly to the worshippers coming in and out of the temple. As he was teaching about Jesus, about his miracles and his resurrection of the dead, several worshippers came and listened to him.

Close to the stone on which Paul was standing was the man crippled from birth. He had been listening intently to the testimony and words of Paul. The Lord's apostle had noticed the man and recognized in him one who had faith and was willing to listen to the Gospel and obey the Lord. He suddenly looked at him. Paul and the crippled man were looking intently at each other — the crippled man surprised by this attention he did not get from anyone.

Continuing to look at him, Paul spoke out with a loud voice saying, ""Stand up!" To the stupefaction of the growing crowds around us, the crippled man jumped up and started walking, first hesitantly and then quickly starting running all over the place. As if startled and afraid, a crowd formed a growing circle around Paul and Barnabas but at a distance. Men and women started running towards the two men from everywhere and from inside the temple of Zeus. Quickly hundreds of people had gathered around Paul, still standing on the large rock, beside Barnabas and the healed man.

A man in the crowd shouted, "These men are the gods Zeus and Hermes in human form who have come back to visit us!" Paul had been speaking and they called him Hermes, because the Greek god in their mythology is the herald and messenger of Mt. Olympus and also the chief god of speech and interpretation. The people believed, through the legendary writings of Ovid that Zeus and Hermes (whose name was Mercury for the Romans) had once visited their area and would come back some day.

As soon as these words were spoken, the priests of the temple came to the entrance of the temple grounds bringing several bulls, as well as wreaths of flowers, so they could worship Paul and Barnabas as the gods they thought had come to visit them.

The two Christian men knew that accepting any kind of worship from men is blasphemy against God and immediately rejected the worship those Gentiles wanted to direct to them saying, "Why are you doing this? We are like you, only human beings!"

As they spoke these words, the priests stood speechless, coming closer to hear them. At that point, they had been keeping distance from the two preachers, as if fearful. They started coming closer to hear what they had to say. Barnabas spoke up and said to them in a loud voice, "Listen friends, we have come here today with Good News. The living God who made heaven and earth, the sea and everything in them is the one you must worship, not us."

As the crowd became almost completely silent, the apostle Paul spoke to everyone, looking all around at all those men and women, "In the past the God who created all things has permitted all the peoples of the earth to go their own ways. But he has never left the peoples without proof of himself. The God who created all things is the one who sends you rain and gives you crops, who gives you food and joyful hearts." (Acts 14.16,17).

As Paul spoke to these men and women, Barnabas was re-minded of the words of the prophet Jeremiah:

> "Can any of the worthless foreign gods send us rain?
>   Does it fall from the sky by itself?
> No, you are the one, O Lord our God!
>   Only you can do such things.
>   So we will wait for you to help us."
> (Jeremiah 14.22)

Seeing that some of the priests were still intent on offer-ing the bulls to worship us, Paul and Barnabas left the crowd and walked towards the city gates where they found a place to rest. A number of those who had been at the temple walked with them wanting to hear more about what they had to say. They continued to tell them about the Lord, about his teach-ings and miracles, his death, resurrection and forgiveness and about eternal life. They preached for several hours as the sun was setting.

When it was almost night, Paul and Barnabas returned to the *mansiones* for the night and after eating the evening meal, went to their room and fell asleep. The next day, early in the morning a group of about twenty Gentiles came to talk with them again. This time four Jewish women and two Jewish boys came with them.

There was no synagogue in Lystra and these Jewish wom-en would gather on the Sabbath day for prayer. Having heard about Paul and Barnabas from some of their Gentile friends, they wanted to hear about their teaching.

The two preachers spent the entire day teaching this group of about forty men and women, both Gentiles and Jews. Among them was a young man by the name of Erastus, who was at that time a servant of Cyrillius, the high priest of Zeus (Jupiter for the Romans).

After resting another night, very early the next morning a great noise plus screams came from outside the lodging. The language spoken was Hebrew. Paul headed to the entrance door of the to meet this small, but noisy group, and discovered they were Jews with a number of Gentiles.

As soon as the apostle opened the door, several of them dragged him out and started throwing stones at him. Protecting his face with his arms the apostle fell to the ground. Thinking he was dead, the group of a dozen men left Paul on the ground and quickly went away. It was later reported that these men were Jews from Lystra and Gentiles from Antioch and Iconium. They had traveled for several days to stop the apostle from speaking in Lystra.

Several of the guests helped carry the apostle into the dining room. The stones had not injured his face or head, but he was in great pain, especially in his lower back. About an hour later, two women and three men came to the door and invited Paul and Barnabas to come and stay in the city. They were from the group Paul had spoken to the day before. They led the two men into the home of one family and took great care of them for six weeks.

Paul and Barnabas were able to teach the two Jewish women and three Jewish men as well as Gentiles who had believed and they were all baptized into the name of the Lord. Paul encouraged them to remain faithful and learn about the Messiah from the Scriptures.

After six weeks and feeling rested, one morning, Paul and Barnabas got ready to depart from Lystra. A large group of disciples came to say goodbye. Among them were two Jewish women and a young boy, whose name was Timothy. The group accompanied the preachers as they left town until they reached the main highway leading to Derbe. The apostle Paul mentioned to these disciples that he and Barnabas would soon be returning to visit Lystra, which gave them much comfort and joy.

20. DERBE

Paul and Barnabas walked for almost an hour on the main highway leading to Derbe. A merchant traveling on a cart and carrying wine offered to take them to the city, which they gladly accepted.

As they visited, this man became interested in the Good News of Jesus Christ and offered to take them to the house of Agapetos, one of his friends, an older man who was a teacher and had studied the Greek philosophers. Agapetos' forefathers had moved from Athens two generations before.

Derbe was a major city in the district of Lycaonia in the Roman province of Galatia. It sat on the major Roman road leading to Lystra, about 60 miles away. The city was important to the Romans since it was in Derbe that all commerce and trade coming from the east and going west was required to pay Roman custom fees.

As soon as they entered the home of this good man, they realized God had opened an amazing door, not just to the home of a friendly host, but to the entire city of Derbe. Agapetos had taught most of his life in Derbe, especially the teachings of Socrates, that had come down through the writings of Plato.

In this home there were no statues of any pagan god. The man had a collection of scrolls neatly placed in one corner of the main room of the house. This was the first time Paul and Barnabas had seen actual writings in any home, with the exception of the scrolls that belonged to the Synagogues or some of the wealthy Jewish families.

That evening they were offered an amazing meal hosted by Agapetos who invited them to spend the night in his home, which was large enough for possibly eight people to live. This invitation was most welcome, since Paul was still in pain from the stoning and the two men were worn out by their travels.

Agapetos was eager to know how all of this happened and why would people want to stone Paul just because he was teaching something different? This started a discussion between Paul and Agapetos, which lasted a good part of the night, concerning the trial of Socrates as recorded by Plato in his book "Apology" written only a few years after the death of the famous Greek philosopher.

In the Apology, Socrates is accused of "not believing in the gods in whom the city believes". It is on this charge that the philosopher was condemned to death. The teacher brought about this discussion as a result of hearing what had happened to Paul, who was almost stoned to death by those who rejected the message about Jesus Christ. Agapetos mentioned to the apostle Paul that Socrates was not only condemned to death for not believing in their gods but also for believing in what Plato calls "other spiritual things" (*Apology 24b*).

During the discussion, Agapetos wanted to know what Paul, a scholar and student of Gamaliel, thought about the accusations that led the leaders of Athens to condemn Socrates to death.

"Socrates was right in rejecting all the Greek gods." Explained the apostle of Jesus. He continued saying, "God who created the world and everything in it is in fact perfectly wise, good and righteous and has manifested himself this way through the creation, through the history of Israel and most importantly in the person of Jesus Christ."

Looking into the eyes of the apostle, as if trying to read deep into his heart, the good man spoke and said: "I know that Socrates taught that man could be like God if he were to emulate the goodness and wisdom of God. True religion, according to Socrates, had only one purpose, which is to improve men's souls; to improve men's souls is the ultimate form of pious worship."

Barnabas took note of how Paul listened with great care to the words of the Greek teacher of philosophy, not interrupting him, but letting the man express his deepest convictions. This keen ability to intently listen was something he had sometimes seen with the great rabbis of Israel, those who had the greatest influence at a deeper level.

The discussion about the *Apology* and the reasons for the condemnation of Socrates continued a good part of the night. The Greek teacher also explained at length how the Greek gods don't agree among themselves as to what is wise and good. His conclusion was that these gods were merely the fabrication of the human mind. They were "gods" made in the image of the man with all the limitations of man. Agapetos laughed at the contradictions between the Greek gods like Zeus and Chronos.

During this conversation, Agapetos discovered aspects of the Jewish Scriptures about creation he had not realized before. The most surprising to him was the important statement found in Genesis that God made everything good, even very good, including man and woman, made in God's image, his resemblance. After about one additional hour of intense discussion, they all decided it was time to rest and went to their rooms.

Agapetos told them the next day that he had decided to open his school for Paul and Barnabas to teach about the Jewish Scriptures, as well as the Gospel of Jesus Christ. They stayed for over three months in Derbe, teaching and preaching.

Every day men and women were being taught and coming to faith in Christ. Agapetos was a good man but but we have not record that he ever came to saving faith in Jesus. Many who were not as educated as Agapetos, and some of them not even able to read or write, came to faith in the promise of eternal life through the resurrected Christ. The message of the cross and the news of Jesus' resurrection made a powerful impact on their lives.

As in all the cities with an important Romans presence, Derbe had for centuries believed and practiced the mystery-religion of Cybele (from Phrygia). Cybele was also called the Great Mother of the Gods and believed to be the god of motherhood. Paul and Barnabas knew that for the Romans, Cybele was called Rhea, and that she was the wife of Cronus and the mother of Zeus.

Cities like Derbe had adopted this goddess because she was believed to protect those who worshipped her. The teachings of Agapetos had attracted those who enjoyed philosophical and literary discussions. A great number of Gentiles remained attached to the gods they worshipped, such as Cybele. These Gentiles chose to worship the patron gods that they believed played a part in their trade or profession. Those who practiced medicine worshipped Apollo. Ceres was the goddess of agriculture and Diana the goddess of hunters.

After a couple of weeks teaching in the school of Agapetos, parents started visiting the school, bringing along their children.

These parents wanted these children to be educated in reading and writing and in the biblical wisdom of the Jewish people, which they had heard about for years. Teaching these children allowed the two preachers to speak to their parents.

Three weeks before their departure from Derbe, Paul and Barnabas met with about twenty Gentiles who had become believers and taught them for several days about the importance of remaining faithful to what they had learned. They also taught these men about the qualifications required of Christian men to be elders or shepherds of God's Church. They were to be men who would be faithful to the teachings they had received and good examples to the whole community and to their families. These recommendations resembled what Paul later wrote in his epistles to Timothy and also to Titus. The apostle Paul also told them that he would be returning to Derbe and the other cities of Galatia and if needed would also write to them.

Three months previously, these men had never heard about Jesus the Savior. These believers also knew that they had brothers and sisters in not too far away Lystra, Iconium and Antioch of Pisidia. They also knew they had brothers and sisters all the way back in Jerusalem and the land of Israel, where the Lord had accomplished his mission.

The gods they had believed in were the creation of the human mind; they were also local in their influence and had evil inclinations. They understood that the God of the Scriptures is the Creator of all things, the Father of the Lord Jesus Christ who is eternal and rules over all the earth and everything else. They also understood that God had spoken to us throughout all time and revealed his will through the Scriptures to be lived out by human beings. They believed Jesus had received authority over all rulers, including the emperor. They understood that they should love one another and treat one another with respect and dignity.

The last worship of Paul and Barnabas with the believers in Derbe happened early in the month of May during the 9th year of the rule of Claudius. A little over one hundred believers gathered that early morning in Derbe for worship and the breaking of bread.

Three brothers had been sent from Lystra to accompany Paul and Barnabas back to that city for safety and protection. They traveled by cart, since they wanted to go back to the cities of Galatia and reach Antioch of Syria before the start of the winter months.

On a beautiful Spring day, over one hundred believers in the Lord Jesus gathered at the gates of Derbe. They all stood by the side of the Roman road leading to Lystra, on which Paul and Barnabas had traveled three months before. Paul and Barnabas prayed over them words of blessings from the Psalms:

> "17 The LORD is righteous in everything he does;
> he is filled with kindness.
> 18 The LORD is close to all who call on him,
> yes, to all who call on him in truth.
> 19 He grants the desires of those who fear him;
> he hears their cries for help and rescues them.
> 20 The LORD protects all those who love him,
> but he destroys the wicked.
> 21 I will praise the LORD,
> and may everyone on earth bless his holy name
> forever and ever."
> (Psalms 145.17-21)

21. ENCOURAGING THE BRETHREN

Paul, Barnabas and the three brethren from Lystra traveled back to Lystra, sixty miles away. They were rejoicing that in each of these cities they would meet new brothers and sisters in the Lord.

Along the way they saw a large flock of goats (several hundred) and some camels grazing in a field. They reached Lystra the same day as the sun was setting. As he walked through the gates of the city, Barnabas remembered how they had come to Lystra through the same gates three months before. A crippled man had been healed in the name of the Lord. Worshippers of Zeus had wanted to offer sacrifices to them, thinking Barnabas and Paul were the gods Zeus and Hermes.

The two preachers had taught some of the idol worshippers gathered close to the entrance of temple of Zeus built along the Roman highway. Later, a few Jewish women had heard about their teaching and had asked to hear them. These women and several Jewish men as well as several Gentile men had come to faith. It was in Lystra that Paul had been stoned by men coming from Iconium. The few women and Gentiles who had believed in Jesus had taken good care of the two preachers and they were able to teach many.

During these three months, more Gentiles had come to faith in the Gospel. Among them was Erastus, the young servant of Cyrillius, the high priest of the temple of Zeus (Jupiter for the Romans). This young man in subsequent years would grow in his faith and dedication and become a teacher in the Lystra congregation.

As they walked through the gates guarded by half a dozen soldiers the two preachers were not even interrogated by the Roman guards. It was already dark when they reached the home of the two Jewish women who had taken care of them on their first visit.

The house of mud and stones was not luxurious but large enough for a few guests. A young man by the name of Timothy was also living in that home with his mother a Jew, and father who was a Greek. The young man came to the door accompanied by an elderly woman, his grandmother, whose name was Lois. The two preachers learned that Timothy's mother name was Eunice. They all spoke the local language, Lycaonian, a dialect of Greek spoken throughout Cappadocia.

Paul and Barnabas left Lystra the early part of July and headed to Iconium. They traveled by cart on the Roman highway towards Iconium and were able to reach the city the same day, since it was only eighteen miles away. The road was broad and well paved, built to accommodate wheeled vehicles.

They had come through Iconium a year before. That is when they had met with Samuel and his family and had attended the Synagogue. At that time, they remained in Iconium for about five months.

Paul and Barnabas reached the gates of Iconium at the setting of the sun. A great number of brothers and sisters in Christ greeted them when they reached the home of Samuel and his wife Rebecca and their family members who had become disciples of Jesus Christ.

Larger than most houses, the main room of Samuel's house was packed with about forty believers, including many children. Three oil lamps gave enough light for a meal to be served and for all of them to see each other. The meal consisted of meat cooked on a brazier, mainly sheep, bread and several wheat-based dishes such as the bulgur-based salad, as well as a yogurt drink that was used almost for every meal. Bulgur was a dish often served in this region. It was made from cracked whole grain and included wheat berries, partially cooked and then dried.

Paul and Barnabas were informed by their hosts that Iconium had seen a lot of unrest after their teaching in the city and their departure. Samuel and Rebecca, well versed in the Scriptures, had been the teachers of the new converts.

A great number of the god-fearing Gentiles who had been attending the large Synagogue of Iconium had become followers of Jesus Christ. This had brought about tension with several of the rulers of the Synagogue. However, the members of the Synagogue were not generally hostile to the believers, since they had known them from childhood and read from the same Scriptures. Both groups rejected the worship of the Greek gods and immoral lifestyle encouraged by the priests and teachers of these pagan religions.

Several Jewish families had turned to Jesus and his teachings. They all continued to meet on the Sabbath at the Synagogue and kept the Jewish festivals. Whether or not the Gentiles should be circumcised and keep all the ceremonial rules of the law remained a subject of tension with some of the Jewish rulers.

Several of the teachers at the Synagogue were angered that the Gentile converts were not being circumcised, as was the custom for proselytes. They also wanted the new Christians to keep the Mosaic laws, especially with clean or unclean foods. This was especially the case since so much of the food, especially meats sold on the market, had been sacrificed in honor of the Greek and Roman gods.

These questions were often raised among all churches established during the missionary journeys of Paul and would be discussed in Jerusalem following his return to Antioch of Syria. The apostle Paul would also write a letter to all these churches of Galatia to confirm and explain, in detail, the decisions of the Jerusalem Council, later reported by Luke (Acts 15).

All around Iconium and throughout the area, streams from the Pisidian mountains made the land on the south-west and south of the city a garden. The day following their arrival, the preachers and brethren met outside by one of those streams that brings water to the land and the inhabitants. They spent the entire day in fellowship and teaching. Samuel and his wife Rebecca, as well as three other Jewish men and a Gentile brother, had been a great example to this large group of disciples and were appointed by the apostle Paul to serve as shepherds and teachers to these brethren.

Paul and Barnabas taught these Christians about the need to remain faithful in the midst of tribulation and opposition as Job had been faithful under trial.

One morning of October, Paul and Barnabas left Iconium and traveling through Antioch of Pisidia headed for Perga and Attalia on the coast, both cities located in the province of Pamphylia. The preachers found a large number of brethren in Perga and were able to teach in that town also. It was in Perga that Marc had left them to return to Jerusalem.

Perga was full of Greek temples and statues dedicated to the Greek gods. After two days in Perga, they left this town with blessings from the church and walked towards Attalia on the Coast. Attalia served as the port of entry from Egypt and Syria to the interior of Asia. It was from Attalia that they would sail back to Antioch of Syria. They covered the twenty miles to Attalia in two days.

The persecution of Christians would progressively increase in that area. Attalia would become a center for the activity of the Imperial priests, who delivered worship certificates to travelers as they offered sacrifices required by the priests to the worship of the emperor. Many travelers sailed from or to Attalia and the Imperial priests watched and checked to see if travelers carried their certificate.

If people were found without this certificate, they were often imprisoned and threatened with death or required to worship the emperor by offering a sacrifice to his statue. When the apostle Paul and Barnabas were traveling and preaching, this widespread opposition to the faith on the part of Rome had not yet occurred.

22. ANTIOCH OF SYRIA

Leaving Attalia, Paul and Barnabas sailed for a little over three days without any storms or obstacles until they reached the port of Seleucia. During their almost two years of travel, they had covered about 1300 miles by land and 500 miles by ship.

It was the beginning of fall when they reached Antioch of Syria, the 9th year of the rule of Claudius, the Roman emperor (49 AD). They landed at Seleucia late one afternoon after days of sailing and ready to finally walk on the land and meet their brethren. It was about noon when they walked through the gates of Antioch. Barnabas could not wait to reunite with his family.

Paul was the guest of Lucius of Cyrene, one of the Christian teachers of the city. Lucius had become a disciple of Jesus in Cyprus after a few brethren had traveled to preach the Gospel in Cyprus following the death of Stephen and the scattering of the Jerusalem Church. (Acts 11.19,20). Lucius was himself the son of a Jewish woman and his father was a Roman citizen.

Barnabas and Sarah had been able to sell most of their farm and land in Cyprus and buy a house in Antioch. They had moved during the early years of the rule of Claudius to work with the churches that now had grown throughout the city and the area. Their move to Antioch from Cyprus was the most important decision they had ever made. Their two sons Samuel and Elijah, at first, stayed in Cyprus and worked on the land. They moved to Antioch two years later.

Antioch in Syria was one of the largest cities of the Roman world with a population of over two hundred thousand. The city, like most other cities in the Empire, had an outside circular wall and at the center, a marketplace. The different ethnic groups who lived in Antioch stayed among their own group and avoided, as much as possible, mixing with other ethnic groups. The city was a main trade intersection between Egypt, Asia, Greece, Italy, and the Land between the two rivers (Mesopotamia). Antioch was also known as, "all the world in one city". Similar to Rome, Antioch contained all the world's richness and diverse populations in one place.

It was in Antioch that the disciples of Jesus were first called Christians, a name we find also in the book of Acts written by Luke. (Acts 11.26; 26.28). In his first letter to believers, the apostle Peter used the name Christian in writing about the sufferings and persecutions they were enduring: "[14] If you are insulted because you bear the name of Christ, you will be blessed, for the glorious Spirit of God rests upon you. [15] If you suffer, however, it must not be for murder, stealing, making trouble, or prying into other people's affairs. [16] But it is no shame to suffer for being a Christian. Praise God for the privilege of being called by his name! (1 Peter 4.14-16)

As Peter himself mentions, in the name Christian, the emphasis is on the word "Christ" which means "Messiah" — a word by which Christians declare Jesus to be their King. These believers were of different ethnic backgrounds but united in appealing to Christ as their Savior and King. Thus the local population started using the word "Christian" to talk about the disciples of Jesus.

Paul and Barnabas reached the large home of Lucius adjoining the city walls on the western side. Barnabas himself lived in the same area and would need to walk only a few hundred feet to reach his home.

Lucius and his wife Deborah, as well as their five children, greeted the two preachers warmly. Lucius had been trained to be a Roman scribe prior to being married to Deborah, a Jewish woman whom he met in Antioch. The Roman scribe was a public notary, a prestigious position among the attendants of the magistrates and paid from the state treasury. Some of the cities of the Empire had all the different ranks of magistrates and attendants paid from the state treasury. As magistrate attendants, the Roman scribes would sometimes assist in religious rituals. Under the rule of Vespasian or Claudius, the Christians in that position were not mandated to perform the religious rituals, especially if they were Jewish or married to a Jewish wife.

This started changing under the rule of Nero, and even more under the reign of Domitian. Most of the Christians who were Romans and in high positions would lose all their possessions and positions with the advent of the rule of Domitian, who mandated the worship of the emperor throughout the entire Empire, under penalty of death.

After greeting Lucius, his family and the brethren, Barnabas walked for about fifteen minutes towards his house, accompanied by Manaen who had been a long-life friend of Herod the Tetrarch. Manaen had become a Christian when the Gospel was first preached in Antioch; he was a good friend of Lucius and worked as a lawyer with the courts.

It was late at night when Barnabas reached the door of his house. He had not seen his family for almost two years. He and Sarah had not been in touch even through letters since Paul and Barnabas never really knew where they would be on their travels and for how long.

When the door opened, Barnabas first saw his son Samuel and his three young children. Beside them stood Sarah, whose beautiful smile he had not seen for so long. The house was spacious, compared to many others in Antioch and had enough space for family members to come and visit, as well as for several guests, if needed. It was built along the western wall of the city, which offered protection from strong winds and cold weather. It had a large flat roof like most other houses in Antioch.

Since their landing in Seleucia, Sarah had already been informed of their safe arrival. Samuel, Elijah and their families had also been informed and were all waiting for the arrival of Barnabas. Manaen, who lived on the other side of the city, would spend the night with them and would accompany them the next day to the home of Lucius, where they would give a report about this first missionary voyage beyond Antioch. The two preachers would recall all that happened in these far-away lands, preaching the Gospel in synagogues and to many Gentiles and seeing Churches being planted on the solid foundation of Jesus the Messiah and Savior of humanity.

Sarah and the wives of Samuel and Elijah had prepared an amazing meal. They all spent a good part of the night eating and rejoicing together for what the Lord was doing throughout the world.

The next day, around the 5th hour in Roman time (about 9:30 a.m.), they were all ready to walk to the home of brother Lucius and quickly reached the large house. Believers had been pouring in the house since early in the morning. When they knocked on the door and it was opened, the main room was already full of Christians.

For a good part of that day, the apostle Paul and Barnabas recounted all that had happened from the time they had left Antioch. Brothers and sisters from all over the city were present that day, eager to hear what the Lord had done. Among them were Simeon called Niger and the teachers and prophets who had prayed as the two preachers were sent off to preach Christ to the world. (Acts 13.1-3).

This all happened in Antioch of Syria during autumn and at the 9th year of the reign of Claudius. Until the Spring of the 10th year of the rule of Claudius, Paul and Barnabas continued to meet with large and small groups of Christians, many of whom were new to the faith and in need of considerable teaching from the Scriptures and about the will of Jesus Christ.

One day early in the spring of the 10th year of the reign of Claudius, two teachers arrived in Antioch coming Jerusalem and asked to be able to speak. The disciples had gathered in the home of Lucius to share in the breaking of the bread and drinking of the wine as a memorial to the death of Christ and his resurrection.

After they had shared in the bread and the cups passed around the assembly, these two men stood up to teach. One of the men, whose name was Samuel, stood up and shared a blessing from the Psalms. The assembly said "amen" to the blessing with one voice. Lucius, Paul and Barnabas listening intently, as well as the church assembled.

These teachers from Jerusalem spoke about how God gave to Abraham the sign of the circumcision after he had called him to leave his country and after he had promised him a son and a large descendance: "9 Then God said to Abraham, 'Your responsibility is to obey the terms of the covenant. You and all your descendants have this continual responsibility. ¹⁰ This is the covenant that you and your descendants must keep: Each male among you must be circumcised. ¹¹ You must cut off the flesh of your foreskin as a sign of the covenant between me and you. ¹² From generation to generation, every male child must be circumcised on the eighth day after his birth. This applies not only to members of your family but also to the servants born in your household and the foreign-born servants whom you have purchased. ¹³ All must be circumcised. Your bodies will bear the mark of my everlasting covenant. ¹⁴ Any male who fails to be circumcised will be cut off from the covenant family for breaking the covenant."' (Genesis 17.9-14)

The teachers continued to speak saying, "In this assembly we have several brothers who have been circumcised as commanded to Abraham our father. Jesus himself was circumcised and so were all his apostles. In Jesus' teachings we see nowhere that the law should be abolished, especially circumcision. Because of this, we implore all of you to understand that the Gentiles who have come to faith in Jesus as their Messiah must also be circumcised in order to be saved and to receive God's blessings as well as eternal life."

Immediately the apostle Paul stood up and responded to this plea with the following words,

"Brethren, listen to the testimony of Scripture. When did Abraham receive the sign of circumcision? Was it before or after he was declared righteous by his faith? We all know it was after. God had already declared Abraham as righteous because of his faith and this is a long time before God gave him the command to be circumcised. What this means is that Abraham's righteousness or salvation in God's sight depended on his faith and not on him being circumcised. We know that God is not God only of the Jews, of those who have received circumcision. He is also God of the Gentiles. The God of Abraham justifies both the Jew and the Gentile by faith since it is written that 'Abraham believed God, and it was counted to him as righteousness". David also declares the blessings of God's forgiveness, not on the basis of having kept the Law but on the basis of God's forgiveness apart from works of the Law." (Genesis 15.6; Psalms 32.1,2).

"We who are of Israel here present have been circumcised as the sign given by God of the covenant between God and Israel, and not as a way to be righteous before God or to receive his grace and mercy. All the Gentiles present here who have never been circumcised are justified and have received salvation by faith in the Lord Jesus and repentance. Now that they have received this salvation and are joined to the Lord, they must not think that they need to be circumcised or follow the Law given to Israel in order to be saved. This would cancel the work of Christ, the need for Him to be our high priest under a new and better covenant." (See Romans chapter 4).

Following these words, there was considerable dissension among the brethren. In his travels, the apostle Paul had met with resistance from Jewish believers coming from the Synagogues, and even Gentile proselytes concerning the status of Gentiles who come to Christ. But this was a different matter, since these teachers were coming from Jerusalem where the apostles had remained up to this time. What did the apostles believe about this? What apostolic teachings would be important concerning this question of circumcision and even of keeping the law of Moses when it comes to Gentiles?

Following this event, the Church in Antioch asked Paul and Barnabas, as well Silas and Titus and a few other teachers to travel and meet with the elders and apostles in Jerusalem concerning this topic of circumcision.

23. JERUSALEM

It would take the group of teachers and leaders from Antioch a little over three weeks to reach Jerusalem, 300 miles away. It was springtime, a perfect season to travel. This happened fourteen years after the apostle Paul had met the Lord on the way to Damascus and had been appointed by the Lord himself as an apostle to the Gentiles. It was also the 10th year of the rule of Claudius.

Accompanying Paul and Barnabas, the group of teachers left Antioch on the road which the Greeks call the "Way of the Sea" or "Way of the Philistines" which takes travelers through Caesarea Maritima, Joppa, Ashkelon and Gaza. The "Way of the Sea" was the most important route from Egypt to Syria, which followed the coastal plain before crossing over the plain of Jezreel and the Jordan valley.

After six days of travel, the group of seven teachers met with the brethren in Phoenicia and from there went into Samaria. They ate and fellowshipped freely with these brethren, who had, for the most part, come from the Gentile world.

Having traveled alongside the apostle Paul for about two years, Barnabas understood that Gentiles are not brought under the old covenant, under the law of Moses, but are brought through their faith and baptism "into the Christ" as Paul wrote in a number of his letters to Christians and churches. In the words of the apostle, they had put on "Christ" and in him there was no difference between Jew or Gentile, slave or free, man or woman: "23 Now before faith came, we were imprisoned and guarded under the law until faith would be revealed. 24 Therefore the law was our disciplinarian until Christ came, so that we might be reckoned as righteous by faith. [25] But now that faith has come, we are no longer subject to a disciplinarian, [26] for in Christ Jesus you are all children of God through faith. [27] As many of you as were baptized into Christ have clothed yourselves with Christ. [28] There is no longer Jew or Greek; there is no longer slave or free; there is no longer male and female, for all of you are one in Christ Jesus. [29] And if you belong to Christ, then you are Abraham's offspring, heirs according to the promise." (Galatians 3.23-29)

Chosen by the Lord as the apostle and teacher to the Gentiles, with all the apostolic authority the Lord Jesus gave him, Paul brought to Jerusalem the truth concerning Gentiles, which he wrote about in his letters.

The teachers entered Jerusalem, coming up the long ascent from Jericho. Jerusalem had been, since Herod the Great, in a constant state of building and rebuilding. Before its destruction by the Romans under the rule of Vespasian (in 70 AD), the city had, besides the temple, palaces and citadels, a theater and amphitheater, as well as several viaducts and many public monuments.

These disciples of Jesus coming to Jerusalem were deeply moved coming up from and around the Mount of Olives. From there, one could see at once across the Kidron valley and set among the surrounding hills, the city of David, the "perfection of beauty", in the words of Lamentations.

The view from the Mount of Olives was dominated by the gleaming gold embellished temple. As they walked uphill, the Christian teachers reminded each other that it was from this place that the salvation of the world was accomplished through the offering of the lamb of God and was now being preached to all nations.

As the travelers approached the city, they were able to see the temple standing high above the old city, at the center point of a huge platform made of white stone. To the south of the temple was the lower city with its yellow brown colored limestone houses and unpaved streets which lead to the Tyropean Valley. The upper city, or Zion, was characterized by its white marble palaces and villas. From here one could see the two large passageways that span the valley, crossing from the upper city to the temple.

They entered Jerusalem through one of its custom stations for taxing goods coming in or out of the city. This is where the tax collectors would be working and checking who needed to be taxed or not.

Since the group of teachers did not carry any goods, they entered the city without having to pay any taxes. That evening, they were the guests of Ben and his family, who had become followers of the Lord and lived closer to the upper city. They were warmly welcomed by over fifty believers who had gathered that evening for a meal and to meet with the teachers. It was an amazing reunion. Paul and Barnabas were asked many questions about their travels.

As they ended the evening, the elders of the Jerusalem Church blessed everyone. Ben blessed these disciples with a Psalm of Asaph whose words were fitting to prepare their minds and hearts for the next day, as they would discuss and teach about the status of Gentiles in the Kingdom of God and his Messiah:

"¹ The LORD, the Mighty One, is God,
  and he has spoken;
he has summoned all humanity
  from where the sun rises to where it sets.
² From Mount Zion, the perfection of beauty,
  God shines in glorious radiance.
³ Our God approaches,
  and he is not silent."
(Psalm 50.1-3)

24. THE JERUSALEM COUNCIL

The next morning, the Christian teachers walked towards the upper part of Jerusalem where they were to meet in a home. They could see from afar the majestic temple. Since the days of Herod the Great, the rebuilt temple after the seventy years of captivity, had been considerably enlarged and refurbished; it was even known as "Herod's temple".

Barnabas was remembering the words of the prophet Jeremiah, words he had learned from an early age as he trained for the priesthood:

> *² Go to the entrance of the* LORD'*s Temple and give this message to the people: 'O Judah, listen to this message from the* LORD*! Listen to it, all of you who worship here! ³ This is what the* LORD *of Heaven's Armies, the God of Israel, says: Even now, if you quit your evil ways, I will let you stay in your own land. ⁴ But don't be fooled by those who promise you safety simply because the* LORD'*s Temple is here. They chant, "The* LORD'*s Temple is here! The* LORD'*s Temple is here!" ⁵ But I will be merciful only if you stop your evil thoughts and deeds and start treating each other with justice; ⁶ only if you stop exploiting foreigners, orphans, and widows; only if you stop your murdering; and only if you stop harming yourselves by worshiping idols. ⁷ Then I will let you stay in this land that I gave to your ancestors to keep forever.* (Jeremiah 7.2-7).

As he was reflecting on the meaning of these words, Barnabas was watching Paul and his dear brothers from Antioch walking ahead of him. *One day,* he thought to himself, *I want to ask*

Paul what he thinks about the temple and how followers of Jesus should view the temple.

After a forty minute walk, the group of teachers finally reached the large house of a disciple who was kin to the family of the high priest. This Christians had come to the faith when the number of disciples multiplied in Jerusalem and many of the Jewish priests came to the faith. (Acts 6.7).

The main room of this large house could easily accommodate over a hundred visitors. All the apostles were present, except James, who had been beheaded by Herod (Agrippa I). This included Mathias, who had replaced Judas. Several elders of the Jerusalem Church were in attendance. The seven teachers from Antioch were warmly welcomed by the apostles and elders. Despite the tensions surrounding this meeting, they all were full of joy to meet with one another in the city of David.

Seventy-five disciples had come to the meeting. A group of about five teachers were sitting together in front but seemed on their guard and unhappy. These teachers had come to the faith from the sect of the Pharisees. They had been teaching for quite some time in Jerusalem and Judea that the Gentiles who come to faith in Jesus as the Jewish Messiah needed to be circumcised and keep the law of Moses to be on right standing with God.

After a prayer and blessing from one of the elders, one of the five brothers who had converted from the Pharisees stood up and spoke to the audience about the importance of circumcision for the Gentiles who come to faith in Jesus. There was really nothing new in what this brother was saying. This teacher and his friends did not seem to see a difference between believers in Jesus and proselytes to Judaism. They believed Jesus to be the Messiah of Israel but also believed and taught that the Gentiles were called by God to enter into the covenant God made with Israel on Mount Sinai. Their conclusion concerning Gentile converts was that "It is necessary to circumcise them and to order them to keep the law of Moses." (Acts 15.5).

In this meeting the apostle Peter spoke up first, followed by Paul and I and finally James, the brother of the Lord.

Peter reminded the assembly how he had been sent by God to speak to Cornelius and his family. They had believed in Christ, had been baptized into his name and had received the Holy Spirit. This was not the first time Peter had reminded these brethren of how Cornelius had come to the faith. From early on, there was a party in the church of Jerusalem known as "the party of the circumcision" that had complained to Peter, saying "you went to uncircumcised men and ate with them". (Acts 11.1,2).

As he had done before, the apostle Peter reminded these disciples how the Holy Spirit fell upon Cornelius and his household as they were listening to the message concerning Jesus and how "[45] The Jewish believers were amazed that the gift of the Holy Spirit had been poured out on the Gentiles, too. [46] For they heard them speaking in other tongues and praising God. Then Peter asked, [47] 'Can anyone object to their being baptized, now that they have received the Holy Spirit just as we did?' [48] So he gave orders for them to be baptized in the name of Jesus Christ". (Acts 10.44-48).

Peter concluded his words, saying: "[10] So why are you now challenging God by burdening the Gentile believers with a yoke that neither we nor our ancestors were able to bear? [11] We believe that we are all saved the same way, by the undeserved grace of the Lord Jesus." (Acts 15.1-,11)

Finally, James the brother of the Lord, rose and spoke, quoting the words of the prophet Amos by which the prophet foretold of the coming of the Messiah who would build back the house of David and call the Gentiles to salvation:

> "16 'Afterward I will return
>   and restore the fallen house of David.
> I will rebuild its ruins
>   and restore it,
> 17 so that the rest of humanity might seek the LORD,
>   including the Gentiles—
>   all those I have called to be mine.
> The LORD has spoken—
> 18   he who made these things known so long ago.'"
> (Acts 15.16,17; Amos 9.11,12)

James concluded his speech by saying that Gentiles do not need to be burdened with the law as a yoke when they turn to God in faith and repentance. He reminded his brethren how Gentiles who, very often, lived in debauchery and immorality should turn away from these practices.

An important and central issue of this meeting was to maintain the spiritual unity of the body of Christ between converts from Judaism and converts from the Gentile world. The believers from the Jewish world were not required to abandon the laws of Moses, the sabbaths or the festivals they had known for generations. On the other hand, it was not required of Gentiles that they should become Jewish in all their ways, including circumcision.

James, the brother of the Lord, knew that the Gentiles needed to turn away from gross immorality and other sins. He also knew that religious pagan practices coming directly from the idolatry of the Gentiles were an offense not only to God but to the Jewish brethren as well, namely the pollution of idols, fornication connected with pagan religions, things strangled and blood. These prohibitions did not imply that other sins such as dishonesty and immorality were permitted but pointed specifically to religious practices such as idol feasts, debaucheries, immoral behavior and the practice of eating blood, which (including things strangled) had already been condemned by God in the covenant with Noah. (Genesis 9.4).

As Barnabas listened carefully to every speech of his brethren, he realized how this meeting in Jerusalem was a teaching appointment needed by the Church; even by the apostles themselves and the entire Church. The meeting confirmed what Paul taught concerning the status of Gentiles who did not need to become Jews to be blessed by God and receive the forgiveness and salvation of the Lord Jesus. Later in his letter to the Galatians, Paul addressed these issues to those he had evangelized on his first missionary journey. He wrote with apostolic authority and opposed efforts to teach Gentiles the need to be circumcised and to come under the law of Moses for salvation.

A letter was written containing these discussions and conclusions and was given to the apostle Paul, to Barnabas and the other teachers who had come from Antioch.

The group of teachers left Jerusalem on a windy and rainy day, rejoicing for all that they had witnessed and heard.

Leaving Jerusalem, they walked for about two hours on the main road that goes from Jerusalem to Gezer and continues towards Antipatris. The thunder became so threatening that they found refuge on the way with a Christian family in Emmaus. This was the town from where two disciples had come and had met the resurrected Lord who spoke to them and also shared the Supper with them. On that occasion they recognized him, as recorded by Luke (chapter 24).

When they reached Emmaus, they entered the warm house of their brethren. They were all completely soaked with the heavy rain. The house was not very large, and the group of teachers was almost too large for the main room of this home. Their hosts at once invited the group into their home despite the small space. There was just enough food for the family of five, but they generously shared whatever they had with these men, demonstrating the beauty of hospitality as taught and practiced by Jesus.

The teachers spent a good part of the night telling these Christians about how the Lord Jesus was being proclaimed all the way to Antioch and beyond into Asia. Their hosts were of Jewish background, and the teachers explained to them what had been decided in Jerusalem.

The teachers rested on the floor of the house which was warm due to the central fireplace kept alive all night.

The next day, the weather was beautiful as the teachers headed towards Antipatris, a town built by Herod the Great, situated about forty-two miles from Jerusalem and twenty-six from

Caesarea. Antipatris was well-watered and located in a richly wooded plain named Capharsaba. This was the town where Paul would later be brought to safety by the Roman soldiers on his way to Rome as he was being threatened with murder. (Acts 23.31-35).

After spending the night in Antipatris the teachers pursued their travels for three days until they finally reached Antioch.

25.   THE CHURCH IN ANTIOCH

After safe travels and finding great hospitality and fellowship along the way, the teachers were relieved to enter through the gates of Antioch of Syria where so many of their brethren were waiting for them, eager to learn the results of their visit to Jerusalem.

It was almost night when they entered Antioch and headed to their homes. Barnabas had been daily praying about their safe arrival and being able to reunite with his family. He was only a short distance from the house and thanked God in his heart: *Lord, I am so grateful to you for my family and these brethren who have traveled with me. May you bring peace and wisdom to the heart of our brethren as they face difficult questions.*

Barnabas knocked on the door. Sarah opened, clearly relieved to see Barnabas since travels were never completely safe. This was the case even on the roads where so many pilgrims would be traveling back and forth from Antioch or Caesarea to Jerusalem.

Barnabas was tired, but that evening had a difficult time falling asleep, thinking about the discussions that would ensue the next day about the status of the Gentiles and the question of circumcision. He had prayed many times for peace of mind but needed to constantly resist the urge to be anxious. As he lay in his bed, he was grateful that Paul had been part of these important discussions.

The next morning, after a short night of rest, the family got ready for the important meeting of the day. Barnabas shared his concerns with Sarah, who encouraged him to rely on God's guidance and comfort through the Holy Spirit and the Lord's promise to always remain present with his disciples until the end of the age.

The Son of encouragement was comforted that his two sons, Samuel and Elijah, would also be present at the meeting on the tenth hour of the next day, about two hours before sunset, after which they would all have a fellowship meal in the evening.

It took Barnabas and his family only twenty minutes to reach the large house of brother Lucius. Born and raised in Cyprus, this disciple became a Christian while he worked as a scribe for the Roman authorities. Applying to be an assistant to the Roman court in Antioch had been a major decision for Lucius. When persecutions against Christians grew years later, especially under Nero and Domitian, Christians like Lucius, who were officials with Rome, lost everything for their faith in Christ and many were put to death for refusing to publicly worship the emperor. It was now the rule of Claudius and there were no such wide-spread persecutions of Christians in the 10th year of the rule of this emperor who would be succeeded by Nero three years later.

The villa of brother Lucius was full of brethren who had come from near and far, mostly from small house churches with only a few family members scattered throughout the city. (Acts 15.30-35).

Paul spoke first and read the letter from the Jerusalem Council to the congregation. Everyone rejoiced greatly because of these teachings. The brethren in Antioch were mostly of Gentile background and it was a relief for them that circumcision was not required to follow Jesus as well as to adopt all the religious ceremonial laws of the Torah. They understood the decision of the Jerusalem council declaring that sexual purity and the rejection of all idolatry were required of all disciples of Jesus of Gentile and Jewish background.

Judas and Silas, who had accompanied the teachers from Jerusalem, also taught well into the evening until the night had fallen and lights needed to be lit in the house. After about three hours of teaching and discussions as well as singing and prayers, all these Christians were ready for the fellowship meal and afterwards rejoiced a good part of the night with many praises and prayers from the Psalms.

26. PAUL'S SECOND MISSIONARY JOURNEY

About ten years prior to these events, Barnabas and Sarah had sold their possessions in Cyprus and had moved to Antioch to work with the Church.

Most of the followers in Antioch were of Gentile background and needed a lot of teaching in the Scriptures. The apostle Paul and Barnabas preached and taught in the city for an entire year until the 11th year of the reign of Claudius, who was emperor of Rome for 13 years (until 54 AD).

On a day when the congregation, meeting at the home of Lucius, had broken bread, the apostle Paul stood up and spoke the following words to the brethren, "It has now been over three years since Barnabas and I have returned from Asia to preach Christ, and churches have been established in many of these towns. It is time for us to return to these areas and visit with these brethren to see how they are doing in the Lord."

Lucius and two of the elders of the Church stood up and asked all of us to pray to the Lord for wisdom and council, as this plan seemed good to them. One of the elders offered the following prayer, "Our sovereign Lord, we come to you for wisdom and council as we believe our brother Paul is right in wanting to return and visit these brethren in Asia."

He ended his prayer quoting from the words of the Psalms:

"Praise the LORD!
I will thank the LORD with all my heart
as I meet with his godly people.

^{2} How amazing are the deeds of the Lord!
All who delight in him should ponder them.
^{10} Fear of the Lord is the foundation of true wisdom.
All who obey his commandments will grow in wisdom.
Praise him forever!"
(Psalm 111).

The next day Paul arrived at Barnabas' house at the third hour to share in a meal and discuss these plans.

The two men had spent many years together in traveling and teaching. Barnabas was looking forward to this great plan of traveling again with Paul and living in the presence of the apostle of the Gentiles, who had met the Lord on the road to Damascus. Knowing that Paul had seen the risen Christ and received from him personal revelation and teaching was always a great source of comfort and joy for him. Being able to listen to the teaching from Scripture brought about by this knowledgeable brother was a constant source of strength and praises to God.

The two men sat at the table giving thanks for the food and praying for God for guidance and strength through the Holy Spirit. Barnabas prayed for wisdom and that the Lord would provide a few companions and teachers for this difficult and perilous journey.

As he ended his prayers, Barnabas spoke to Paul saying, "We will need help and should encourage my cousin Mark to join us in this journey, as well as others. What are your thoughts about this?"

"My brother" said Paul laying his hands on the shoulders of Barnabas as he did sometimes when an important decision needed to be made, "Yes, we will need help on this journey. I am thinking of taking Silas with us, who was present with us in Jerusalem at that important meeting we had with the elders and apostles. His witness will be important and though, still young, he has taken a very significant part in teaching, not only in Jerusalem but here in Antioch."

Barnabas responded saying, "Well, I am completely in agreement to take Silas. His knowledge of the Scriptures and understanding of the Gospel of Christ cannot be doubted as well as his ability to teach. And we should also ask Mark to accompany us on this journey."

"We should not ask Mark to come with us this time", replied the apostle Paul.

Barnabas was completely taken by surprise at these words of Paul. He knew his cousin Mark to be zealous for the cause of Christ and known for his faithful life of discipleship over many years. So, Barnabas responded saying, "Brother Paul, you know my cousin Mark and how devoted he is. I know this will be so encouraging to him and he will be a great asset to our journey."

Having said these words, Barnabas thought to himself *I know Paul will understand the importance of taking Mark with us.* However, Paul did not immediately respond. He was thinking deeply. Was he hesitating or praying in his heart on how to respond? Paul was never someone to react quickly. When he had reproached Peter and Barnabas for hypocrisy when they refused to eat with brethren who had been converted from the Gentiles, he did this with great calm and strength, as if following exactly the words of the prophet Isaiah, "In quietness and confidence is your strength." (Isaiah 30.15)

Finally, after a time of silence that seemed unending to Barnabas, Paul spoke up with a great calm and eyes full of compassion, "My dear brother, we cannot take Mark with us because this time we will need him to remain with us until we finish visiting all these churches. The journey will be long and full of perils; we will need to pursue our travels without interruption, if possible. So, it is my conviction that we need to take Silas with us, who Peter especially has recommended to me as a faithful brother. As we travel this time, we will certainly face growing hostility from the Romans, whose policies are slowly changing against the churches and the brethren. I have been informed of how the possible successor to Claudius will be Nero and we already know that he will bring havoc to the faith and the brethren."

For the first time since they had traveled and worked together, Barnabas was not certain that the apostle Paul was right in his judgment about Mark. Paul and Barnabas continued to disagree strongly over the question of Mark.

It was with deep sadness that Barnabas said good night to Paul as he left the house and returned to stay with Lucius his host. That night Barnabas cried to the Lord and shed many tears over the question of Mark. He decided in his heart that he would go his own way with Mark while Paul would travel with Silas.

Three days later, Paul and Barnabas, as well as Lucius and others met to pray and make plans for this next important journey into Asia. Paul and Silas would travel into Asia while Barnabas would choose Mark as a co-worker, first in Antioch and then ask him if he would accompany him to Cyprus, since Paul would not be returning to the island but would travel first to Tarsus by land.

On the next Friday morning, a great number of brethren accompanied Paul and Silas as they departed on the road that leads from Antioch to the Cilician Gates north of Tarsus and from there to Derbe and beyond.

The Spring morning was crisp, almost cold, as the two men left Antioch and their brethren with many tears and prayers. None of them knew at the time that this journey would take Paul and Silas beyond Asia and into Macedonia and Achaia.

None of them knew that many would come to faith in Christ throughout these regions and that this journey would last almost three years, up to the last year of the rule of Claudius, who would be replaced by Nero. And none of them knew that in Lystra, Timothy would be joining the apostle Paul and Silas or that Luke would join the apostle and his co-workers as they were about to enter Macedonia.

Sarah and Barnabas began discussing how they could serve the Lord in the future, especially since they were getting older. The Church in Antioch now had many capable teachers and preachers. One evening after their meal and having prayed together, they decided to ask the brethren to pray about their future. They wanted at the same time, to seek advice from some of the more mature men and women in Antioch and Jerusalem.

They both believed that before making any decision, it was best to first pray and seek God's wisdom and direction. They also believed that wise and mature men and women of God should pray for them and if willing, give them advice.

They also wanted to talk to their two sons about the future. Samuel and Elijah and their wives, as well as many brothers and sisters, started praying diligently for God's direction for Barnabas and Sarah.

One morning, a few days later, a courier came with a letter all the way from Macedonia. Eliezer and his wife Esther were writing to Barnabas explaining their plans soon to return to Cyprus. They still had land on the island and would gladly give some land to Barnabas, if he needed it.

Having read this letter, Sarah and Barnabas looked at each other and understood right away that God was giving them the response they were looking for concerning the future. The Church in Cyprus had very few capable teachers or preachers of the Word. It was time for them to return to Cyprus and work with the existing churches now and worship on the island.

The following day, Barnabas and Sarah met with brother Lucius and asked for a meeting in his home concerning these plans. This happened on Sunday, as they brethren met to break bread in memory of the Lord's death and resurrection.

Mark had returned to Jerusalem and was continuing to write his account of Jesus' ministry and teachings. Barnabas wrote a letter to Mark asking if he would join him in this teaching mission to the Cyprus churches. Three weeks later, Mark arrived in Antioch, and they made preparation to travel to Cyprus.

During the second week of September, on a Tuesday, Barnabas and Sarah as well as Mark, Samuel and Elijah, with their families and a great number of the brothers and sisters, headed to Seleucia on the coast. The merchant ship they planned to board would head to the southern side of Cyprus, a trip Barnabas had often made.

27. BACK TO CYPRUS

About twenty years before the birth of Jesus, Cyprus became a senatorial province of Rome, divided into four districts. Paphos on the western side of Cyprus and Salamis on the eastern coast were the centers of the Roman administration.

The island had always been known as a peaceful place, and this was the reason why so many wealthy Roman citizens had built villas on Cyprus. There were no Jewish revolts in Cyprus like the ones that developed under the rule of Nero in the 12th year of his reign. In the fall of that year Jewish rebels had expelled the Romans from Jerusalem and set up a revolutionary government. Vespasian (who would later become emperor) was sent by Nero to crush the rebellion. He was joined by Titus (who also would be one of the emperors) and at that point the Roman armies then entered into Galilee ready for war. This Jewish rebellion led to the fall of Jerusalem and destruction of Jerusalem, including the temple, four years later. The fortress of Masada resisted for three years before being conquered by Roman general Flavius Silva.

The Roman rulers did not, at first, care about the followers of Christ. This political policy lasted until the rule of Nero and later Domitian, whose policies became more and more aggressive towards Christians who would not worship the emperor. The Roman rulers wanted to be worshipped as gods and this folly led to greater opposition and persecution against the Christian faith from the pagan religions and pagan priests.

As Barnabas and Sarah, as well as Mark traveled to Cyprus, they talked about what was going on in Jerusalem and the news coming from other parts of the world. They also talked about the fact that it was now well known by the brethren in Jerusalem that the Lord Jesus had chosen Paul to be His apostle to the Gentiles, not only as an evangelist, but also as a teacher of what the Lord had revealed to him.

During the general Jerusalem Council with the apostles and elders, the authority of the apostle Paul was confirmed, as well as the right hand of fellowship given to him by the existing apostles. The Church in Jerusalem was in agreement concerning the question of the status of Gentiles or Jews, as they came to faith in Christ.

At the same time, Rome was growing weary of the rebellions in Judea which were the result of heavy taxation and corruption of the rulers chosen by Rome. Clashes between Jewish rebels, especially the Zealots, and the Romans, were occurring more often year after year.

Mark mentioned that he had learned much from Peter, with whom he had had many conversations. This relationship with Peter would be important for him as he wrote his Gospel account of Jesus' teachings and miracles, as well as His death and resurrection. According to Mark, Peter wanted Barnabas's cousin to continue serving the Lord as an evangelist and travel where the Lord would lead him to preach Christ crucified and resurrected.

On the ship, Mark had long conversations with the captain who was from Greece and seemed favorable to his words, being skeptical about the existence of the Greek gods and their religion. The sailor enjoyed the accounts of Jesus' ministry, given by Mark, such as calming the storm on the sea of. Galilee, of Jesus walking on water (Mark chapters 6 and 14).

They sailed on the Great Sea with surprisingly calm winds until they reached the coast of Cyprus. The ship captain informed the passengers that the ship would land on the southern coast of Cyprus, at Amathus, ancient city near Limassol, among sandy hills and sand dunes and founded by the Phoenicians (about 1500 BC). From Amathus they would travel east along the coast to Kition and finally all the way to Salamis.

Barnabas and Sarah could not wait to see their good friends, Eliezer and Esther, who had settled back in Salamis two years previously, after living in Greece for over fifteen years.

As the three of them finally disembarked at Amathus, the presence of the Romans was immediately felt. Each important city, all the way to Paphos the capital, was filled with the majestic theaters, official buildings as well as large villas built for the Roman rulers.

As Barnabas looked towards the east as far as he could see, he remembered how he had traveled the same Roman road along the southern coast of Cyprus, going the opposite direction towards Paphos in company of Paul. Sergius Paulus, the Roman governor, had become a believer in the Lord.

As they travelled, they often prayed together for Paul and Silas, who were now traveling together through Asia. They also prayed for all these Christians and Churches they would be visiting, as well as for the local Gentile populations – hoping that these populations would be welcoming to the Good News of salvation through Jesus so that the Kingdom of Christ would continue to grow throughout these regions and even the world.

Mark was grateful to accompany Barnabas to Cyprus but had always wanted to go and preach the Gospel to places like

Alexandria and even Rome. He was fully devoted to sharing the Good News with everyone he met, and he took to heart the great mission given by Jesus to the Church prior to his ascension: "I have been given all authority in heaven and on earth. [19] Therefore, go and make disciples of all the nations, baptizing them in the name of the Father and the Son and the Holy Spirit. [20] Teach these new disciples to obey all the commands I have given you. And be sure of this: I am with you always, even to the end of the age." (Matthew 28.18-20)

It took the three of them almost eight days to reach Salamis. Eliezer and Esther had settled back in Cyprus and their land was large enough for a herd of over a hundred goats and some sheep. They were able to make goat cheese that was sold all over that part of the island and the sheep were mainly for meat.

As they came close to Salamis, Barnabas and Sarah recognized the familiar hills and even olive trees here and there which were still producing olives in the land they had sold many years ago.

The Roman road reached the gates of the Salamis, recently built for protection but also for greater control on the part of Rome. With greater control came a growing presence of the worship of the Roman gods.

Mark, Sarah and Barnabas walked through the Southern gates of Salamis and after half an hour came through the northern gates. In front of them on a hill stood the farm Eliezer and Esther had built after their return from Greece.

After going through Salamis, they saw on their left, about a mile away, the hill on which their farm once stood, but was now replaced by a stately villa belonging to the governor's family.

This governor resided most of the time in Paphos but used this villa as a vacation home for himself or special guests.

Close to the emperor's villa stood the temple recently built and dedicated to the worship of Dionysius. Dionysius was feared and was considered a threat by most pagans. Of course, as a non-existent god, he was not really a threat but as the apostle Paul had written to the Christians in Corinth, he was only the appearance or disguise for what the Greeks call "demons" and the Hebrews call "shedim" – spirits of destruction and death. Christianity taught that these spirits are behind the false gods worshipped by the pagans (1 Corinthians 12.20; Psalms 106.37 and Deuteronomy 32.15-18).

Eliezer and Esther, as well as their twin daughters, were members of the Salamis synagogue. Their son, Jonathan, was living and working in Corinth as a legal scribe. The twin daughters, Rebeka and Abigail, were now seventeen years old and living at home. They were tall like their father, gracious and hospitable like their parents.

Sarah and Barnabas had often prayed for their friends, not certain how to help them understand the Gospel of Jesus, crucified and raised from the dead, who would one day return to judge the world. But in this work of evangelism, their trust was in the Lord and the work of His Spirit and not in their own ability or power to convince the hearts of men and women. As taught by Jesus, they saw themselves as sowers and waterers of the Gospel. They knew that God, through the work of his Spirit, could bring the human heart to faith in Jesus as Messiah and Savior. They also knew that God has granted the freedom to choose, the freedom to accept or not the truth about Jesus, the Lord and Savior.

That evening the weather was still quite warm and the door to the house was wide open. They all embraced each other with a warm welcome, since they had not seen each other for so many years. Eliezer was still tending the flock and would return home soon. They talked about what had happened in their families and in their lives. Esther knew that Barnabas and Sarah had become believers in Jesus as the Messiah and surprisingly this did not seem to be a difficult issue for her.

Eliezer arrived at sunset just in time for dinner. He did not seem to have grown any older. His hair was still black, and he appeared to be as strong as ever. Barnabas thanked God in his heart for Eliezer's friendship and for his good health.

They all talked for a good part of the night. Mark, who had been an eye witness to Jesus during his ministry, talked about the Savior and answered many questions Eliezer and his famly had concerning the biblical Messiah.

Eliezer informed everyone that the new governor was a dedicated worshipper of Dionysus and many of the other Greek gods.

Barnabas knew that Paphos had a congregation of Christians and that there were also brethren in some of the other smaller towns such as Kition, Limassol and Kourion, all located along the southern coast. Travelers usually preferred traveling to the southern coast, which could explain why Christians had settled there or that others had heard the Gospel of Christ in those areas.

As Barnabas listened to his friend Eliezer, he thought to himself, *"I am now an old man and there are more temples than ever, built in honor of Zeus."* These temples often had phrases engraved at their entrance such as "ΕΛΘΕ ΖΕΥ ΒΑΣΙΛΕΥ ΘΕΩΝ ΑΡΙΣΤΕ ΗΔΕΕ ΜΕΓΙΣΤΕ" (meaning "Come Zeus who is the greatest of kings, the most perfect and the most gentle."). Barnabas thought *What do these inscriptions mean by "gentle" when describing Zeus, the cruel father of Athena, Apollo and Artemis and known to be without any pity?*

28. EVANGELISM

The return of Barnabas and Sarah to Cyprus took place while Vespasian was still emperor. The apostle Paul was coming to the end of his second missionary journey; he visited the churches in Galatia that had been established on the first missionary journey. He then continued into Macedonia and Greece.

After short time with Barnabas on Cyprus, Mark left for Egypt. Mark had been writing down an account of Jesus' life as the Messiah of Israel. Part of this account had already been written in Jerusalem. It was in Egypt that Mark continued to write his Gospel account, which would be the first one completed and circulated among the early churches. For several years, the presence of Mark played an important role in the evangelistic work of the early Church since Mark, without being an apostle, was an actual witness of Jesus' ministry and had been close to the apostles, especially to Peter.

The temple of Dionysus, the god of wine and festivity, stood on the land which Barnabas had sold many years previously to help feed the Christians in Judea (Acts 4.37). It had been built by the new governor who lived in Paphos on the western coast of Cyprus. The Romans used to call this god "Bacchus". Even though Dionysus was worshipped in Cyprus, his main worship according to Euripides was centered at Mount Kithairon in central Greece. Dionysus was part of the twelve Olympians, which included, among others, Zeus, Poseidon and Artemis.

Homer and Hesiod, among others, provided genealogies of the gods and why they needed to be honored and worshiped and what were their spheres of jurisdiction. All aspects of the lives of human beings were under the control of all these gods, as well as patron gods of different professions. The gods of Greece and Rome were also used for vows and oaths.

Instead of believing in the one and only Creator, as found in the Jewish Scripture,s the Greeks and others made gods of all the elements of creation: Chaos, Ge (earth), Erebus (darkness), Aether (air and day), Uranus (Sky) were gods. All of these and hundreds of others had unique powers and could either bless or curse; either help or hurt.

From the time God called Abraham out of Ur of the Chaldeans and throughout the remaining Scriptures, God had given a revelation of His blessings through Abraham and his posterity — blessings that would extend to all the "families of the earth". The LORD had said to Abram, "Leave your native country, your relatives, and your father's family, and go to the land that I will show you. [2] I will make you into a great nation. I will bless you and make you famous, and you will be a blessing to others. [3] I will bless those who bless you and curse those who treat you with contempt. All the families on earth will be blessed through you." (Genesis 12.1-3).

In the book of Genesis, the first man (Adam) and first woman (Eve) had been created in the image of God. They enjoyed the presence of God in the garden. Jesus often taught about the importance of what God did and said in the "beginning". This was the case when discussing the question of marriage and divorce: "Haven't you read the Scriptures?" Jesus replied. "They record that from the beginning 'God made them male and female.'" [5] And he said, "'This explains why a man leaves his father and mother and is joined to his wife, and the two are united into one. ⁶Since they are no longer two but one, let no one split apart what God has joined together." (Matthew 19.4-6)

In the Genesis account, man and woman had lost their position in relation to God and sin had separated them from the glory and presence of the eternal and gracious Father. Jesus taught that sin makes slaves of all human beings: "I tell you the truth, everyone who sins is a slave of sin." (John 8.34)

All of this needed to be taught to the pagans. In their missionary travels, Paul and Barnabas had, at times, preached directly to the pagans, even though their teaching was mainly centered in the Synagogues. In Cyprus, the greatest challenge for Christians was the religion and gods brought there by the Greeks. During the rule of Nero, the Roman administration and political control grew significantly on Cyprus, especially with the Jewish rebellions looming in Judea and Syria.

Since their move to Antioch from Cyprus, many things had changed for Barnabas. His land had been sold. He was grateful that Eliezer and his family had a place to live on land that was formerly his. His former employee had sufficient resources to be able to buy and sell produce from his small farm.

Barnabas and Sarah were now living as neighbors to their friends. The small house was large enough for them and to have some guests, when needed. Hospitality was very important for traveling brothers and sisters, and for evangelists and teachers sent out by the churches.

The temple of Dionysus, recently built and close to Salamis, meant a growing presence of the worshippers of this god, mostly Roman men, who were given to orgies and sexual licentiousness.

In his travels, Barnabas had met a few Gentiles who had been seeking wisdom and a life of discipline. Sergius Paulus, the Roman governor of Cyprus, had been one of them. He had come to the Lord upon hearing the preaching of the Gospel but the present governor over Cyprus was a worshipper of Dionysus and was completely given to lust, as well as the love of money, fame and power.

Barnabas and Sarah knew that the work laid before them would be difficult. They would need to be in prayer constantly, with complete faith in the working of God and His Spirit, as they strove diligently to bring the Gospel of salvation and sanctification to the inhabitants of the island.

The rebellion in Judea had been terrifying for the people of Israel. All of Jerusalem had been destroyed in great part and the temple was gone. Thousands of Jews had been taken captive and scattered throughout the Empire.

During these events, the apostle Paul had traveled and gathered workers who preached the Gospel with him, establishing churches throughout the Greek world. The Church of Christ was now present, in its earthly form, all around the Great Sea, extending from Alexandria to Rome.

The Son of encouragement had heard of the great persecutions the Christians were enduring in Rome. and some other centers of Roman rule. Christians were not in rebellion against Caesar or in opposition to the Roman rulers or legions. Followers of Jesus struggled against the pagan gods and their ways which lead men away from a godly life, from the true love of God, of neighbor and the blessings of God.

Barnabas recalled the words of Jesus and the teachings of Scriptures about the dangers of false gods, of evil spiritual forces at war with God, of sinful behaviors which bring about anguish and spiritual death to human beings, as the apostle Paul had written about in his letter to the Ephesians: "**2** Once you were dead because of your disobedience and your many sins. ² You used to live in sin, just like the rest of the world, obeying the devil—the commander of the powers in the unseen world. He is the spirit at work in the hearts of those who refuse to obey God. ³ All of us used to live that way, following the passionate desires and inclinations of our sinful nature. By our very nature we were subject to God's anger, just like everyone else." (Ephesians 2.1-3)

29. CHRIST AND DIONYSIOS

When Barnabas and Sarah returned to Salamis, the two temples built in Paphos and Salamis in honor of Dionysius, had become big attractions for the inhabitants of Cyprus and visitors to the island. The worship of this Greek deity had become widespread within the local population. The inhabitants of Cyprus were under the impression that if the governor worshiped Dionysius, it would be good for them to do the same. They believed that by worshipping this god they were pleasing those who ruled over them and thus would reap benefits for themselves.

The temples dedicated to the worship of Dionysius were also "houses" with a central court, a main worship room and many other rooms. They were full of mosaics describing Dionysius and many other mythological deities of the Greeks. The cult of Dionysius (Bacchus) involved the drinking of wine and obscene sexual practices. The worship of this god was emphasized in December-January when the vines were pruned. Later in January-February, the *Lenaia* festivals were held; the end of March saw the festivals of the *Dionysia*. After that, the *Eleusinian* mysteries (secret practices) were held between the end of September and the beginning of October with mostly wine drinking and orgies.

The Greek and Roman god were also patron gods of most commercial and business activities. The worship of the patron gods had become a growing source of opposition and persecution for followers of Christ. Christians were losing their livelihood for their refusal to worship the Greek and Roman deities and to go along with the sinful and immoral practices connected to this worship.

After the reign of Vespasian came the short rule of Titus, followed by the rule of Domitian. Barnabas and the church in Cyprus heard from Christians in Rome that this emperor was like a "second Nero", but even worse. Whenever he appeared in public, he wanted to be worshipped and proclaimed as "Lord and god".

During the second year of Domitian's rule, the new coins minted by Domitian and used for trade depicting the head of Apollo and a raven, were used for most business transactions. The emperor consulted with Apollo, the Roman god of music, poetry, as well as light and knowledge of the future. The raven on the coins reminded everyone that the emperor also consulted with the "raven"; the Romans believing that the flight pattern of the bird could help predict the future.

At the beginning of the rule of Domitian, the governor of Cyprus had organized a grand tour of the Island in order to encourage the worship of the emperor and also of the gods worshipped in Rome by the emperor.

Before this grand tour of Salamis, the governor had sent several spies throughout the land to prepare a report of what was happening among the populations. These kinds of reports would often make their way to Rome. The content of these reports would either benefit the governor or hurt his reputation and position. Gone were the days of governor Sergius Paulus, a man who had been open to the teachings of the Jewish Scriptures and who believed the Gospel of Jesus Christ.

Barnabas knew that his brethren were now living in a completely new era and this change had happened rather quickly: in less than one generation. It seemed to him that the members of the synagogue in Salamis and the Christians were the only ones to see the danger of the new policies of Rome bent on forcing everyone to comply to the folly of one man who considered himself as a god to be worshipped.

A day came when both the Synagogue worshipers and the Christians in Salamis were solemnly ordered to appear before the governor and his lawyers. Eliezer, Barnabas and others had discussed what all of this meant for their beautiful island and for its population and how they should respond.

Would it be possible to speak to the governor and present to him their plea to worship only one God, the God of Abraham, of Isaac and Jacob? Could they hope to convince this man of God's warnings concerning sin and the judgment to come?

30. LUCIUS HEARS THE TRUTH

Lucius had been preparing himself a good part of his life in Rome for his appointment as governor of Cyprus. He came from the Bruttia family (or "gens") who were well known in Rome, since the late republic. None of the members of the Bruttia family had obtained important magistracies until emperor Titus appointed Lucius to be governor of Cyprus at the age of forty. Lucius was married to Fulvill and they had one son, whose name was Caius Bruttius Praesens.

The order for the Christians in Salamis to appear before the governor was given during the second year of the rule of Domitian. This emperor seemed to be born with a natural inclination for cruelty. He first slew his brother, and in his rage put to death some of the Roman senators, in many cases, to confiscate their estates. The persecution of Christians followed and quickly reached Jerusalem, where the bishop Simeon had been crucified upon orders of the emperor. By his sole authority, Domitian had declared into imperial law that, "No Christian, once brought before the tribunal, should be exempted from punishment without renouncing his religion."

The persecutions against Christians had largely increased due to the number of informers, who for the sake of gain, swore away the lives of the innocent. Many of the most faithful and dedicated brethren had been put to death. Many were willing to fabricate and spread rumors against the followers of Christ. If there was a famine, pestilence or earthquake inflicting any of the Roman provinces, the blame was quickly laid on the Christians for refusing to worship the Roman gods and the emperor.

The policies of Rome against the faith and disciples of Jesus had been increasing and gradually reached the once peaceful island of Cyprus. It had become unlawful to even mention or pronounce the name of Jesus of Nazareth or speak about him to anybody in public. The worshippers of Dionysius on Cyprus had grown bolder with their threats, day by day and week by week, towards both the synagogue and the Christian brethren.

It was in the second year of Domitian's rule, on the day of preparation (Friday), that leaders from the Salamis Church were to have a hearing with Lucius, accompanied by his lawyers. Asked to be present to represent the Church were Barnabas, Denys, Protasius and Gervasius.

Originally the meeting was to be held in one of the rooms of the house of worship of Dionysius. Barnabas and the brethren requested not to meet in that location because it was so close to the worship of this false god, as well as the orgies and sexual practices involved in the worship of the Greek god. They were able to convince the governor's lawyers to have the meeting simply in the regular Roman court at the center of Salamis. The argument that the court was a more solemn place for this hearing convinced the governor to change his mind.

The court, like most Roman official buildings, had a Greek look due to the inclusion of the Corinthian columns in its design. Marble covered the walls of the two major court rooms. Words in honor of Augustus, the first of the Roman emperors, were engraved in large letters on the wall in front of where the governor and his lawyers sat: RES GESTAE DIVI AUGUSTI QUIBUS ORBEM TERRARUM IMPERIO POPULI ROMANI SUBIECIT ("The exploits of the divine Augustus, by which he brought the whole world under the rule of the Roman people"). These words were destined to impress all who came into this court for a hearing. The emperor saw himself as a god and a mediator between the people and the gods, a sort of supreme priest (*pontifex maximus*) between men and the gods. The governor and his lawyers saw themselves as the protectors of the people and of their interests. The law was on their side and in their eyes there was no other law higher they needed to take into account.

During that important meeting, the governor did not speak first. The final decision, however, would be left to him. The lawyers would be first to argue the case for Rome and for the emperor concerning the worship of the gods of Rome and the emperor.

The four men entered the court room and were told to stand while the titles of the emperor were proclaimed by one of the lawyers. After they sat down, facing the three lawyers and the governor, one of the lawyers made a solemn proclamation, saying, "Citizens of Cyprus and of the great Empire under our lord and god Domitian, we want to extend understanding to you, friendship and benevolence, which are virtues we Romans have always held as very important."

Another lawyer continued with the following words: "It has come to the attention of our honorable governor Lucius Bruttia Maximus, the highest authority in the land, that you are speaking in public about one Jesus you call the Christ or king. We are here to explain to you how such speech is against the laws of Rome and an insult to our god and lord the emperor. Do you have anything to say?"

Since Barnabas was the older man present, a native of Cyprus and an elder of the local Church, he knew it was his turn to stand up and respond. Barnabas stood up and proclaimed the following words: "Our lord and Savior Jesus, when he was before Pontius Pilate, was asked the question if he was the king of the Jews. Jesus then responded with these words: 'My kingdom is not of this world. If it were, my servants would fight to prevent my arrest by the Jewish leaders. But now my kingdom is from another place.' To this Pilate responded, "You are a king then?". This is when Jesus responded saying: 'You say that I am a king. In fact, the reason I was born and came into the world is to testify to the truth. Everyone on the side of truth listens to me.'

Barnabas continued, saying, "Pilate, in conclusion to this encounter with our master said: 'I find no basis for a charge against him'. Now these things happened under emperor Tiberius. Pilate, who knew the Roman law, did not find that the claims or teachings of Jesus were a threat to Rome or in opposition to the Roman laws. The reason for this is that Jesus had come as the king of a kingdom 'not of this world' but rather a kingdom ruled by truth."

In response to these words of Barnabas, upon a sign made by the governor, a third lawyer stood up and said, "You can worship your Jesus and read his teachings in your times of worship on certain days, but our governor has ordered all Christians on this island not to be public with your beliefs. Our governor is showing his great mercy towards you by letting you worship Jesus in the privacy of your meetings on the days set for these meetings. This is the case, both for the Jews and their synagogues, and you Christians, who are another Jewish sect who worship a man crucified under Roman law. We could also ask you, how it is that you men who are able to think, read and speak, could believe and hope in a man who died as a criminal, according to our laws."

This was followed by a brief silence of a few minutes. At this point, Lucius the governor, stood up and spoke to the seven men saying:

"As the governor of this Roman province, I am here to represent the will of the highest authority, which is the emperor, who presently is Titus Flavius Domitianus. Our divine and honorable emperor only answers to the gods of Olympus and is, like I am, a worshipper of Bacchus. What our emperor declares as law, is what ought to be done; our law needs to be obeyed by all who live under the Roman jurisdiction. Are you willing to disobey such a powerful being, a true god and representative of the Roman people?"

After a brief silence, the Christian Denys who had been trained in the Greek schools of philosophy, stood up and spoke to the governor and his three lawyers saying:

"Honorable governor, for hundreds of years people have worshipped the God of Abraham, Isaac and Jacob, who created the world. They have worshipped God who called Abraham in Babylonia, under the rule of the Persians and now under the rule of Rome.

"We Christians and Jews worship this God, who is not an unknown god as some worship in Athens and other places. We worship the Creator of the world, who is above all gods and all kings as was recognized, even by the great king Nebuchadnezzar, who ordered all to worship the Creator, after God healed him and brought him back to his senses. We worship the God who saved the people of Israel from the cruel Persians, who wanted to destroy us all. We also worship the God who delivered us from the cruel persecutions of the Syrian rulers who succeeded Alexander the Great, which the Romans fought and conquered.

"The Christians here also worship the God of Abraham, Isaac and Jacob, as testified by Barnabas, whose ancestors have lived in Cyprus for many generations. We all worship the God who rules in heaven and is above all gods because He created the world. For many generations, the Roman Republic and the emperors have been kind to those who worship the God of Abraham, Isaac and Jacob and never thought they should forbid people to pray or mention God in public.

"Whether they are Jews or Christians, these people believe in all the virtues taught by many of the Roman writers that you yourself have read and studied. Are not these virtues, such as courtesy, friendliness or industriousness extoled by the best of your philosophers? Are they not to the advantage and benefit of those under your rule? These are all virtues taught by the prophets of Israel, by Jesus, an Israelite and by the Christians in the world and here in Salamis."

After Denys' long speech, which only a brief summary is mentioned here, none of the lawyers spoke up or responded. They were all looking at Lucius as if waiting for his response.

After a silence which seemed very long, Lucius asked the four Christians to stand up. He said the following words: "I will have to defer to the emperor and his counsel. I proclaim and let it be recorded on this day the following: As long as the Christians under my jurisdiction abide by the great rules of our

Roman wise men, as long as they live peacefully and do not commit murders, they are to be left at peace and not troubled in any way. We will need to meet another time when I receive answers from Rome, from the emperor and his counsel. You may go in peace."

Eliezer, Barnabas, Denys, Protasius and Gervasius left the courtroom after what seemed to them a very long time but lasting only a couple of hours. Each one of these men had a family and each one knew how dangerous the situation had become for them and their families, as well as the Church.

Deep in thought, Barnabas walked back home, realizing that once more the future was not guaranteed in the sense of safety and peace for his family and friends, as well as for his brethren. He went back in his mind to the times in his life when he had to step out in faith, not knowing what the next day would bring. Walking alongside his friend Eliezer and the three younger men of Gentile background, he knew how they felt, without having to inquire. He knew that their first thoughts were for their wives and children and the dangers that loomed ahead.

That same day Barnabas invited a number of brethren to his home, accompanied by their wives and children. He had something to share with them which would bring great joy and encouragement to all of them.

31.   A GREAT GIFT

Three days prior to the meeting with the governor and his law-yers, two brethren had come all the way from Antioch to visit with Barnabas and Sarah. They had brought with them a great and precious gift: a copy of the Gospel as written by Mark, who had completed his Gospel in Egypt. Mark was now an older man, like Barnabas, and had been teaching and preaching in Alexandria for many years.

At sunset Denys, Protasius and Gervasius came with their families to the home of the "Son of encouragement". There were now eight adults in the small dwelling with an additional nine children from the ages of three to thirteen. Barnabas and Sarah had prayed about this important event of present-ing the scroll of Mark's Gospel to these disciples. They had rejoiced ever since they had been informed months before of this great gift coming from the church in Antioch. Now was the time to read from Mark's account concerning Jesus the Christ.

Barnabas was sitting on one of the few chairs in the house. The adults sat on the raised platforms that faced the entrance door and the children sat on cushions spread on the ground. Sarah brought in the scroll of Mark's Gospel made of sever-al papyri sown together to form the scroll. Barnabas started reading:

This is the Good News about Jesus the Messiah, the Son of God. It began [2] just as the prophet Isaiah had written:

> "Look, I am sending my messenger ahead of you,
>   and he will prepare your way.

³ He is a voice shouting in the wilderness,
  'Prepare the way for the LORD's coming!
    Clear the road for him!'"

After this reading, Barnabas spoke these words, "After his baptism by John the Baptist, our Lord preached throughout the land of Israel, saying: "¹⁵ The time promised by God has come at last!" he announced. "The Kingdom of God is near! Repent of your sins and believe the Good News!" (Mark 1.15).

Barnabas continued to read the entire account of Mark's Gospel until the very end of the scroll. There was not one interruption during this reading. Tears were flowing from the eyes of all present that evening. Barnabas then offered a prayer of blessing and thanks and invited everyone for a fellowship meal which lasted almost two hours. Everyone had questions about what they had heard from Mark's account of the Gospel of Jesus Christ.

After the meal, Barnabas spoke again, saying:

"The kingdom of God is now offered to men and women as a gift from God, if they receive it by faith, turn away from their evil and sins and give their hearts and lives to the Lord. This is the message we have been able to tell many here in Salamis — many who live in fear of the gods, especially the god Dionysus. As you know, a month ago, the Lord opened a door so we could preach the Gospel to those in the population steeped in the worship of Dionysus.

"At that time, three teachers from Athens came to Cyprus to meet with some of leaders of Salamis and the Roman authorities about opening a school of learning in Greek philosophy and mythology. These men were sent from Athens by the school of the Stoics. Zeno, the founder of the school, was mostly inspired by the teachings of the Greek philosopher, Socrates. Socrates exhorted his disciples to seek wisdom and virtue, above everything else, even above money and pleasure. Socrates himself demonstrated humility by stating the fact that he was not always certain about what was virtuous. The stoics emphasized the importance of looking at one's own failures and lack of understanding."

Gervasius spoke up and said, "The teachings of Jesus and of the Scriptures, such as Proverbs, are all about this importance of seeking wisdom and virtue above all else. This is what I discovered when invited by a friend of mine to one of Rome's congregations. This is how I was first introduced to the teachings of Jesus."

"Yes, responded Barnabas, Thank you brother for reminding us of this." He added: "The three stoic teachers invited the population to the main courthouse where we were only a few days ago confronted by Lucius and his lawyers. Over one hundred men and women came to hear about these teachings. Most of those present were worshippers of Dionysus. After speaking to the crowd, the three Greek teachers allowed any who were present and who wished to speak up or ask questions. I had spent a lot of time in the company of the apostle Paul and others who had preached to the Gentiles who were inclined to philosophy. I stood up and asked the following question: 'I understand and respect what you teach about the important virtues necessary for living a good, righteous and fruitful life and I agree that these virtues are of the highest importance, especially the virtue of examining our own lives.' I continued saying, "There are many in this place who worship the god Dionysus, as if he will reward those who acknowledge his power. What can you say about the virtues of this god?"

"After a moment, one of the three philosophers spoke up and said: 'The gods of our Greek fables are the product of our own minds and express our deepest human passions. Their stories are not given to teach us virtues or a better way to live. It is only in the pursuit of wisdom and through self-examination that we can learn what the virtues are and contribute to a better world."

Looking intently at his brethren and the young people present that evening, Barnabas said the following words: "This philosopher was saying what our Jewish prophets had said, which is that the pagan gods do not even exist. They are not real and do not teach us anything that can be useful for our lives. In this, the philosophers from Athens stood in opposition to the priests of the temple of Dionysus and those who benefit in popularity and in material goods from the worship of this false god."

Barnabas continued his account concerning the visit in Salamis of the Greek teachers of philosophy and said, "About fifty of those who attended this meeting of the Greek philosophers from Athens came to me afterwards and wanted to speak with me. So, we invited them the next day to learn about the wisdom of the God of creation through the Scriptures and in the person of Jesus Christ.

"Early in the morning of the next day, our small meeting room for the Church was packed with so many that everyone except some of the elderly needed to stand. The Greek teachers continued the discussion of the previous evening concerning the need for virtues and wisdom, as taught by Socrates and others. Others who had been invited were surprised to learn that they were worshipping a god, Dionysus, who was only a legend, like those mentioned by Homer.

"We presented to them the life and teachings of Jesus of Nazareth, who was the Savior promised to Israel for hundreds of years. Those who had been invited and even the Greek teachers were amazed that Jesus healed the sick and brought back the dead to life. They were touched by how he was treated by those who rejected him and how he died on the cross.

"These guests listened with amazement about the account of his resurrection from the dead. We assured them that all this was not legendary but came from reliable witnesses, some still alive, like Mark. The Greek teachers did not seem convinced by our witness concerning Jesus Christ, but our other guests continued to ask questions and wanted more information about the life of Jesus, his unusual death and resurrection.

"There were also questions asked about the worship practices taught in the Scriptures and to the Churches. The god Dionysus was just as immoral as any human being and did not mind lying or killing, if necessary. So, it was important for us to talk about the Lord's commandments concerning evil practices found in the world of the Greeks and Romans."

"Jesus wanted purity of heart and righteous behavior from his followers. This is why Jesus started preaching about "repentance", which is a change of heart, of mind and behavior; a turning away from sinful behavior to actions that give honor to God and dignity to man."

"After a long discussion with these men and women, we offered a meal for those who wanted to stay and continue to talk.

Over half of those present stayed for the meal and wanted to hear more about Jesus Christ. But the others had heard enough and left our house. We sang to the Lord and prayed as we blessed the food. It was a beautiful and memorable moment. There was great joy seen on the faces and in the smiles of those present.

Barnabas finished his long speech with these words, "On that day, twenty-three precious souls came to faith in Jesus our Lord and to repentance. Sarah and I had known some of these knew Christians since an early age. We were now brothers and sisters and shared in the same hope of eternal life through the Lord Jesus."

32. OVERCOMING FEAR

After that long day and memorable meeting that continued well into the night, the twenty-three new believers left the house of Barnabas. The family was finally able to rest for what would be a short night.

Early in the morning, while the family was still resting, Barnabas left his home and walked up the familiar hill to the place where he could enjoy the sight of the Great Sea at the rising of the sun. Some days, a ship could be seen. Barnabas would then remember his travels with Paul. Barnabas missed the presence of the dear apostle. *How would the apostle deal with his own fears and the fear that had started gripping his brethren in Cyprus? What words would he find to comfort and strengthen them? What words would he say? What prayers would he pray?*

Paul had gone to his reward years ago. Some of his letters were circulating among the churches, including the one to the churches in Ephesus and Colossae and his letters to the evangelist Timothy. Barnabas had memorized the content of these short letters. He recalled the words of Paul written in his second letter to the evangelist Timothy.

"⁸ Always remember that Jesus Christ, a descendant of King David, was raised from the dead. This is the Good News I preach. ⁹ And because I preach this Good News, I am suffering and have been chained like a criminal. But the word of God cannot be chained. ¹⁰ So I am willing to endure anything if it will bring salvation and eternal glory in Christ Jesus to those God has chosen.

[11] This is a trustworthy saying:

> If we die with him,
>   we will also live with him.
> [12] If we endure hardship,
>   we will reign with him.
> If we deny him,
>   he will deny us.
> [13] If we are unfaithful,
>   he remains faithful,
>   for he cannot deny who he is.

[14] Remind everyone about these things, and command them in God's presence to stop fighting over words. Such arguments are useless, and they can ruin those who hear them." (2 Timothy 2.8-14)

Deep in his heart, Barnabas knew how blessed he and Sarah were to be able to shepherd and encourage the Church of Christ in his homeland before departing from this world for the heavenly dwelling prepared for the faithful.

His prayers were always an occasion to express his gratitude. He never forgot how many years ago he heard the Good News and met the apostles of Jesus; how he was able to be part of the great work of evangelism and building up of the Church, the body of Christ in this world.

His sons, Samuel and Elijah, and their families were living in Antioch. Mark was in Egypt and had written a Gospel account of the life and work of Jesus. Barnabas and Sarah had moved back to Cyprus at the end of September during the last year of the reign of Vespasian. That was three years ago.

Now Domitian was the ruler in Rome. This emperor was like another Nero. He wanted to be worshipped as a god himself and for the past two years had been extending this policy over the Empire. This attitude and behavior of the ruler in Rome had emboldened the worshippers of Greek and Roman deities. Even some who had been friendly, some who would never have thought of harming the Christians, were going along with this policy of opposition to everything Christian, especially the message of Jesus as the judge and ruler of the universe.

All the apostles had gone to their reward, except for John, who lived in Ephesus and was still a shepherd and teacher to the Churches in Asia. Barnabas remembered the words of John quoting Jesus: "I am the light of the world. If you follow me, you won't have to walk in darkness, because you will have the light that leads to life." There was darkness all around, but this light of Jesus was growing all over the world and would grow in intensity until He would return in glory.

That morning, the Great Sea was as calm as the sun rising in its majesty, seemingly unmoved by anything happening on earth. A calm that contrasted with the thoughts battling in the mind of the Son of encouragement. Birds were chirping as usual. It was all so delightful and would normally bring joy to the heart of Barnabas, but the future looked bleak. Possibly in a matter of weeks, the life of his family and his brethren would be turned around.

Barnabas remembered the day Mark first described to him the life and work of Jesus and invited him to break bread with the believers and apostles in Jerusalem; how he began to see the Messiah in a different light — a Messiah who came to serve and save humanity.

A few years ago, before his death at the hands of Nero, Paul had written several letters to the persecuted brethren scattered through the Empire. He wrote to the saints in Ephesus a letter which was quickly circulated, first to the many communities around Ephesus and then all over the Empire.

In this letter, the apostle Paul reminded Jesus' disciples that the main battles in life were with spiritual forces and not against human beings. In his letters, the apostle taught that no authority and no power are above Christ; that he rules over all rulers and powers and will be returning for the great day of judgment and resurrection of the dead.

"[19] I also pray that you will understand the incredible greatness of God's power for us who believe him. This is the same mighty power [20] that raised Christ from the dead and seated him in the place of honor at God's right hand in the heavenly realms. [21] Now he is far above any ruler or authority or power or leader or anything else—not only in this world but also in the world to come. [22] God has put all things under the authority of Christ and has made him head over all things for the benefit of the church. [23] And the church is his body; it is made full and complete by Christ, who fills all things everywhere with himself." (Ephesians 1.19-23)

That morning, Barnabas prayed for over three hours. He rose up and started walking down the hill to his house. He kept in his heart the sight of the Great Sea with its beautiful changing blue colors as the sun shone mightily on the waters. This was a piece of the good world God had created, which reflected His graciousness, the beauty and harmony of His will.

As he walked downhill, Barnabas breathed deeply, enjoying the smell of the many varieties of flowers on his way home.

Barnabas thought to himself, *my homeland is such a beautiful place, and I am grateful to God for this gift. Difficult times lie ahead, but we can still enjoy the beauty of His creation, the truth of his Word and the warmth of Christian brotherhood. We can be deeply grateful to God, who so loved the world that he sent his own beloved Son to live the life of a humble servant. He died for everyone to reconcile us to God who made all things and will judge all people.*

These are the thoughts and words he would soon be sharing with the congregation, as the brethren would meet for fellowship and the breaking of break.

IV

THE THREE ENVOYS DEPART FROM SALAMIS

Barnabas had ended his account.

The envoys from Lystra: Erastus, Lucius and Justus, had listened all day to the Son of encouragement, with just an interruption for some food. They had continued to talk to Barnabas well until dawn.

As the day was ending and it was getting dark, disciples started arriving at the house of Barnabas, which was also where the Church met for worship. The place was too small for the growing congregation and only some of the brethren were able to come that evening to visit with the three envoys from Lystra. Twenty-two Christians came that evening to share in a meal and speak with the brethren from Lystra.

They all came with a heavy heart, but willing to pray and praise the Lord despite growing opposition. Some of the Christians who had been worshippers of Dionysios were present that evening. They had come to faith a few weeks before the visit of the three Christian leaders from Lystra. The brethren had shared news from Lystra. The Roman opposition to the faith had, at the time, a limited impact on southern Galatia. The three brothers from Lystra had learned about the behavior of the new emperor, mostly during their visit to Cyprus and would return to inform the churches in Lystra and the surrounding area.

Late into the night, the brethren who left the house of Barnabas said their good buys to the three men from Lystra, with tears and prayers for their safe return home the next day.

V

THE SETTING OF THE SUN

The three envoys sent from the congregation of the Lord in Lystra had brought a gifting contribution to aid the struggling church in Salamis. This contribution would help some of the poorer members in Salamis, especially the widows, but also some of the brethren recently converted to the faith who had been expelled from the local professional guilds also called "colleges" in Rome, placed under the protection and blessings of patron gods.

Patron gods held authority and power over professions and occupations. Hermes for pilots, Hephaistos for blacksmiths and Aphrodite for prostitutes and other sex workers within the religious contexts of Rome and Greece. Many places in Cyprus were linked to ancient gods and legends such as the Stone of Aphrodite or the Baths of Aphrodite and Adonis or Mount Cassion.

Those who had come to faith in Jesus and had turned away from the worship of the many Greek and Roman gods and had been ostracized from the guilds and had lost their source of income. The funds brought by the Lystra brethren would help these men and their families.

***

Since the departure that morning of Erastus, Justus and Lucius and their return back to Lystra, Barnabas had been praying and fasting most of the day until dawn. Now 76 years old, he watched as they slowly walked away. The pain of their departure brought tears to the eyes of the old man until there were no more tears to shed.

Beautiful as usual with colors ranging from red to orange and finally yellow at the level of the water, the majestic sun was slowly setting over the Great Sea, reflecting in its own unique way the majesty of the Creator.

Six months before, twenty-two worshippers of Bacchus had come to the faith, which had infuriated the high priest of the cult, as well as the governor of Cyprus, himself a worshipper of the god.

The leaders of the Church had spoken recently to the governor and his lawyers in defense of the Church accused of sedition against Cesar. For a final decision on the matter, the governor had appealed to Domitian.

Barnabas walked slowly down the hill to the small house which was also where the congregation met for worship, as well as prayer and study.

The night came swiftly over the land. As usual, the waves of the Great Sea crashing on the beach nearby produced the only sound that could be heard.

That night everything seemed so quiet and so soothing, while men full of hate against Jesus and his disciples were meeting secretly to kill Barnabas at the most opportune time.

They were wishing the death of one who had been known by so many as "the son of encouragement" and who remained an encourager until his last moments. The death of one whose heart and life had been transformed by the power of the Holy Spirit and the Good News about Jesus the Christ, the Victor over death and over sin.

These hateful and violent men concluded that the best place and time to kill Barnabas would be on an occasion when he was invited to speak in the local Synagogue; this way the blame would fall on the Jews.

And thus, it happened as they planned.

The last words of Barnabas spoken on that Sabbath day at a conclusion of his teaching were words from a Psalm of David:

> [5] Let all that I am wait quietly before God,
>   for my hope is in him.
> [6] He alone is my rock and my salvation,
>   my fortress where I will not be shaken.
> [7] My victory and honor come from God alone.
>   He is my refuge, a rock where no enemy can reach me.
> [8] O my people, trust in him at all times.
>   Pour out your heart to him,
>   for God is our refuge. (Psalm 62.5-8)

About the Author

Yann Opsitch is an author, minister, teacher and evangelist to the nations. He is the director of l'Ecole du Maître (School of the Master), an online Bible training program for Christian leaders living in the French speaking world. Yann studied at the North Ireland Bible School, University of Geneva (Switzerland), Abilene Christian University, University of North Texas.

Yann is the author in English of: *Let Us Come Before His Presence: 365 Days to Learn, Meditate and Pray from the Psalms and the Sermon on the Mount* and *Dialogues on Revelation with John the Apostle.* He is the author in French of *Paroles du Christ sur la Montagne, En Esprit et en Vérité, La Sagesse et l'Adversité, Le Cœur et l'Invisible, Le Dieu de la Création et de la Révélation.*

If you enjoyed this book, please consider leaving an online review. The author would appreciate reading your thoughts. All of Yann's books are on Amazon.

Visit the author's website at https://yannopsitch.com/

You can also follow the author on social media at:

Instagram: @yannopsitch

Twitter: @opsitch.

Facebook: https://www.facebook.com/yannopsitch

Linkedin: www.linkedin.com/in/yannopsitch

Acknowledgments:

My gratitude to my wife Rita and to Kathy Chesshir for reading the manuscript and for great advice prior to publication. My gratitude to Ioana Muller for the illustrations.

www.ingramcontent.com/pod-product-compliance
Lightning Source LLC
Chambersburg PA
CBHW060411310726

48976CB00003B/1016